SPINDRIFT ISLAND

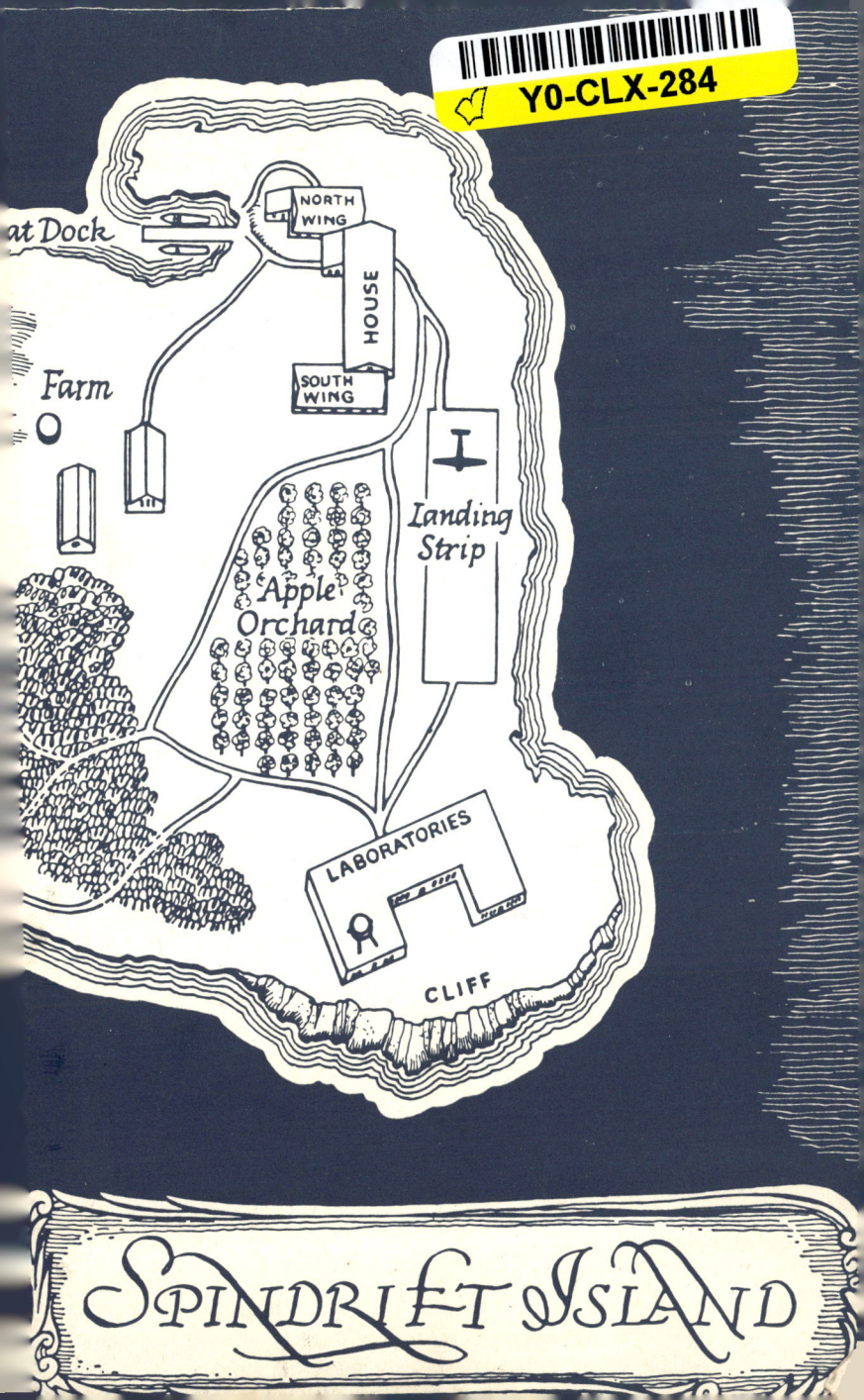

THE ELECTRONIC MIND READER

The Rick Brant Science-Adventure *Stories*

BY JOHN BLAINE

———•‑•‑•———

THE ROCKET'S SHADOW
THE LOST CITY
SEA GOLD
100 FATHOMS UNDER
THE WHISPERING BOX MYSTERY
THE PHANTOM SHARK
SMUGGLERS' REEF
THE CAVES OF FEAR
STAIRWAY TO DANGER
THE GOLDEN SKULL
THE WAILING OCTOPUS
THE ELECTRONIC MIND READER
THE SCARLET LAKE MYSTERY
THE PIRATES OF SHAN
THE BLUE GHOST MYSTERY

Horrified with fear, the men threw themselves to the deck

A RICK BRANT SCIENCE-ADVENTURE STORY

THE ELECTRONIC MIND READER

BY JOHN BLAINE

GROSSET & DUNLAP PUBLISHERS

NEW YORK, N. Y.

© BY GROSSET & DUNLAP, INC., 1957

ALL RIGHTS RESERVED

Printed in the United States of America

Contents

CHAPTER		PAGE
I	The Million-Dollar Gimmick	1
II	The Invasion of Spindrift	10
III	A System Within a System	24
IV	A Haircut and a Wink	33
V	JANIG Runs a Security Check	45
VI	A Calm Precedes a Storm	55
VII	The Peripatetic Barber	65
VIII	The Mind Reader Strikes	74
IX	Dagger of the Mind	86
X	Search for Strangers	94
XI	The Dangerous Resemblance	105
XII	The Coast Guard Draws a Blank	119
XIII	The Megabuck Mob Acts	130
XIV	Surveillance—with Cereal	148
XV	A Matter of Brain Waves	154
XVI	The Vanishing Mermaids	164
XVII	Pointer to Disaster	179
XVIII	The One-Man Boarding Party	186
XIX	Taped for Trouble	194
XX	JANIG Closes In	202

THE ELECTRONIC MIND READER

CHAPTER I

The Million-Dollar Gimmick

Rick Brant stretched luxuriously and slid down to a half-reclining, half-sitting position in his dad's favorite library armchair. He called, "Barby! Hurry up!"

Don Scott looked up from his adjustment of the television picture. "What's the rush? The show hasn't started yet."

Rick explained, "She likes the commercials."

A moment later Barbara Brant appeared in the doorway, hastily finishing a doughnut. Rick cocked an eyebrow at her. "If you're going to eat, you might at least bring a plateful, so we can have some, too."

Barby gulped. "Sorry. I didn't intend to have a doughnut. I went to the kitchen to see if Mom and Dad wanted to watch the show, and they were having doughnuts and milk."

"Never mind," Scotty said. "We forgive you. We'll get ours later. Are Mom and Dad coming?"

"Maybe later. Now be quiet, please, so I can hear the commercial."

Dismal, the Brant pup, wandered in and paused at Rick's chair to have his ears scratched before taking up his favorite position, under the TV table. Rick obliged and the shaggy pup groaned with pleasure.

"Why all the interest in a breakfast-food commercial?" Scotty asked.

"The announcer is cute," Barby stated.

This made no sense to Scotty. He stretched out on the rug in front of the set, then rolled over on his back and looked up at the girl. "I don't get it. Then why do you eat Crummies for breakfast instead of the hay this guy sells?"

"The Crummies announcer is cuter," Barby explained patiently.

The boys grinned and fell silent as the cereal salesman went into his spiel. Barby perched on the edge of a chair and listened attentively.

Rick watched his sister's expressive face, chuckling to himself. Barby always listened to the commercials. It was only fair, she insisted, and the boys went along with her wishes. Come right down to it, Rick thought, listening to commercials was the price that had to be paid for entertainment. Not listening meant not paying the price. He didn't think that the point was particularly important, but there was a small element of justice in Barby's view.

Their Sunday evenings on Spindrift, the private

island off the New Jersey coast, usually ended with this particular program. The members of the Spindrift staff were not TV enthusiasts at best, and they cared little about the program. Mr. and Mrs. Brant sometimes watched, more for the sake of being companionable than for the sake of the program. But usually the three young people watched alone.

The program was a typical quiz. Contestants who were expert on a particular category returned week after week on their build-up to a grand prize, which was a quarter of a million dollars. This quiz, however, had elements that the younger Brants liked. In the first place, the contestants were ordinary people. The producer didn't seem to go in for odd characters as other programs did.

For the past few weeks the hero-contestant had been an eighteen-year-old coal miner from Pennsylvania. There was nothing unusual about him, except for one thing: he had become interested in the mining of precious stones, and from there he had studied their history. He was an expert on historical gems.

Now, as the master of ceremonies greeted the miner, Barby said with admiration, "He has a wonderful personality. And imagine him knowing so much about gems!"

Rick draped a leg over the chair arm. "See, Scotty? The perfect reaction."

"What do you mean?" Barby demanded indignantly. "He absolutely does have a wonderful personality, and I think it's amazing that a coal miner should know so much about gems."

Scotty grinned up at her. "Rick means people can't get on quiz shows unless they have good TV personalities. And how much appeal would the show have if a gem expert answered questions on gems?"

"I see what you mean," Barby agreed.

"That's it," Rick nodded. "Anyway, I agree that the miner has a swell personality, and he certainly knows his gems."

The three fell quiet as the quiz began. The questions were really tough, filled with the kind of detail no one could be expected to remember, but which good contestants always did. Then, at a crucial moment, the miner hesitated over identification of a date in the long and bloody history of the Koh-i-noor diamond.

"If only we could help him," Barby wailed.

"We don't know, either," Scotty reminded.

But Rick suddenly realized that they did know—or, at least, had the answer available. He was certain it could be found in one of his father's books, if not in the encyclopedia. But even if they had time to look it up, which they didn't, the contestant couldn't hear them in a soundproof booth. Or could they get a message to him if they were part of the studio audience? Or was there some other way? It was typical of Rick, when faced with an apparently insoluble problem, to look for an answer.

The miner finally remembered, and the three

breathed a mutual sigh of relief. But the ordeal was not yet over, because the questioning had several parts. Next came a quiz on the Star of Africa.

The questions asked, the camera began switching from the contestant's face to the tense faces in the audience. A woman, probably the miner's mother . . . a man with a beard . . . a man with a hearing aid . . .

Rick suddenly sat up straight. He had it! He knew how the information could be handed to the contestant! At least he knew in theory. He sat back and started to work out the details.

The miner made it. Limp and happy, he came out of the booth, shook hands with the MC, and staggered off with an armload of books containing answers to next week's series of questions. The announcer went into the final commercial, with Barby and Scotty listening attentively. Rick didn't listen. He had a wonderful idea on which he was putting the finishing touches.

As programs shifted, Scotty reached up and turned off the set. Dismal left his place under the table and trotted off to the kitchen.

"Me for a doughnut," Scotty announced.

Barby was still spellbound by the miner's success. "It's just fantastic, utterly, how much he knows." She shook her smooth blond head. "I wish I knew that much about something."

"Want to win a million?" Rick asked.

"Who doesn't?" Barby returned dreamily. Suddenly she stared. "You have a Look on your face," she stated. "Rick Brant, you're cooking up something!"

Rick grinned. "I can win the quiz," he said casually. "It's easy. Let me know if either of you want to win. Of course you might end up in jail if you're not real careful, but I think it'll work."

Scotty looked his disbelief. "Easy, huh? What are you expert on?"

"Nothing," Rick said airily. "And anything. Of course we all know you're an expert on eating, but that's not a category, it's a capacity."

Barby gave what might be described as a ladylike sneer.

Rick shook his head. "It's terrible the way people in this house have no faith in genius. Just terrible." He sighed heavily.

Scotty watched him suspiciously. "All right, Doctor Brant. Give with the great idea."

"Okay." Rick waved at the encircling shelves of books. "Pick a subject. Any subject, so long as it is contained in a very few references. Like the life of the bee, or the Adventures of Sherlock Holmes, or the Life of Dickens."

Barby said obligingly, "All right. I pick Ben Franklin. Now what?"

"We get the major books on old Ben, plus the copy of the encyclopedia we need. Then we set up an index, and we put principal categories of information on file cards. For Ben, we'd need the Sayings

THE MILLION-DOLLAR GIMMICK 7

of Poor Richard, and the dates they appeared, and where. And we'd need a list of his inventions, plus dates. And so on. Generally, we fix things so we can find any answer in a few seconds."

Barby shook her head. "That would be awfully hard. It would take weeks, and whoever operated the file would have to know it nearly by heart."

Rick agreed. "But isn't a million bucks worth a few weeks of effort?"

Rick's famous father, Hartson Brant, walked into the library in time to hear the last comment. His eyebrows went up. "What's all this megabuck talk?"

That was a new word to Barby. "What talk?"

"In the metric system, 'meg' means million. So a megabuck is a million bucks, if you'll pardon the slang."

"Oh—well Rick is going to win a megabuck."

Rick explained rapidly about choosing a subject that could be cross-indexed for ease of reference, then went on. "After we get the subject all set, we choose the contestant. It has to be a real person. We'd need several contestants, because the gimmick could be worked on every big money quiz. Maybe more than once on each. Of course the contestants would have to be members of the Megabuck Mob, as we'll call it."

"I like that," Barby said enthusiastically. "That would make me a Megabuck Moll, wouldn't it?"

"Yep," Scotty agreed. "And Rick can be the Megabuck Mole."

"And you can be the Megabuck Moose, you big ox," Rick finished. He was warming up to his subject now. There had to be a hole in it somewhere, but he hadn't found it yet. "Anyway, we have Ben Franklin on file cards and Barby has studied carefully to be the first contestant. Then what?"

"Someone asks who Ben Franklin was, and I say that he started a chain of department stores," Barby said helpfully.

"Not you," Rick denied. "You know all the right answers. And why? Because the Megabuck Mob is behind you. The Megabuck Moose is going through the cards, and the Megabuck Mole is feeding the answers into the Megabuck Memory Machine, and the Megabuck Moll in maidenly modesty mumbles madly—"

"Help him," Scotty interrupted. "His lips are stuck together. He can't say anything but mmmmm."

But Barby was interested now. "And how does the Memory Machine madly machinate and murmur the answers?"

"Mmm," Rick murmured. "That is the secret!"

Hartson Brant threatened his son with a handy volume of the Physics Handbook. "Out with it, young man. This is no time to keep secrets, now that we're all partners in the deal."

Rick sighed. He waved at Barby. "Look at her. So young, so smart, so pretty. But the poor girl has a very slight handicap. She has to wear a hearing aid . . ."

Scotty got it then. "Hey! Rick, that's great! The hearing aid would be a radio receiver!"

Barby got it, too. She finished in a rush, "And the Megabuck Mob would be watching on TV, and digging out the answers, and the Memory Machine would be a radio transmitter . . ."

"It wouldn't matter about the soundproof booth," Scotty chimed in, "because radio will go right through the walls!"

Hartson Brant held both hands to his head in mock horror. "To think that my only son should turn out to be a halfway criminal genius!"

Rick glanced up at his father suspiciously. "Halfway?" He knew from the word that the scientist had immediately spotted some reason why his gimmick wouldn't work.

"Never mind, son." Hartson Brant put a hand on Rick's shoulder. "The Megabuck Moll can bake you a cake with a file in it, so you can break out of jail. I'm sure you won't mind being a fugitive from justice."

A harsh growl from the doorway caused them all to whirl around, startled. "He'll never get a chance. The Megabuck Mob is pinched as of right now. The federal government is taking over this island!"

Crouched in the doorway, submachine gun cradled in his arms, was an officer of the United States Coast Guard!

CHAPTER II

The Invasion of Spindrift

HARTSON BRANT reacted first. He said severely, "I've tried to teach Rick that one never points a firearm at people. You're setting him a bad example." Then the scientist smiled and held out his hand. "This is an unexpected pleasure, Steve. Why didn't you let us know you were coming? And why the disguise?"

Steve Ames, a chief agent of JANIG, the Joint Army-Navy Intelligence Group with which Spindrift had so often worked, straightened up and grinned. He winked at the astonished young people. "Hi, gang."

The trio chorused, "Hi, Steve."

Steve shook hands with Hartson Brant, then explained, "I'm not really setting a bad example. If you'll look closely, you'll see that the bolt of this chopper is open, the safety is on, and there isn't a round in the chamber."

"But why carry it at all?" Barby demanded.

Rick closed his mouth. He had been about to ask the same thing. He felt a tingle of excitement. When Steve Ames showed up on Spindrift, adventure wasn't far off. The federal agent came to Spindrift only for help, and then only when his usual sources had failed.

The first time, in the case of *The Whispering Box Mystery*, the Spindrifters had worked with Steve in Washington. Recently, quite by accident, the boys had become involved in a JANIG case while vacationing in the Virgin Islands. As the case of *The Wailing Octopus* came to an end, Steve had warned them that he might see them soon. And now here he was.

"The reason for the chopper is a long story," Steve answered Barby. "But the reason for the uniform is simple. It's mine."

Then Steve, who had never before appeared as anything but a civilian, was actually a full Commander in the Coast Guard! Rick marveled at how little they really knew about their friend. He certainly excelled at keeping his mouth shut. Probably he was a reserve officer.

"I think you look handsome in it," Barby said dreamily. The boys had kidded her before about getting all misty-eyed when Steve showed up. Actually, Steve was a very handsome young man, so Barby's mild crush was understandable.

"That makes it worth wearing," Steve said gallantly. Barby beamed.

Hartson Brant detached a key from his chain and handed it to Steve with a flourish. "You said you were taking over the island, I believe? You'll need the house key."

Rick smiled. That was his father's way of leading the conversation back to Steve's reason for coming, without taking the edge off their delight at the unexpected reunion. But Steve was not to be pushed into business talk so easily. He looked at Rick.

"You and your schemes! I think I'll poke it full of holes just to show you that crime doesn't pay."

Scotty asked curiously, "How much did you hear?"

"The whole plan. I've been casing the joint, as we say. Okay, Rick. You must have considered that a rash of winners wearing hearing aids would attract attention and comment. How are you going to prevent it?"

Rick answered automatically, his mind not really on his Great Idea any more. So Steve had been "casing" the island! He replied, "Not all the hearing aids would be visible. For instance, I could make a receiver for Barby that would be an ornamental plastic band to wear the way girls wear barrettes, or whatever they call them. Or, I could fit a receiver into a special pair of glasses. There's one type of hearing aid that's built into glasses, you know."

"I do know," Steve agreed. "All right. I'll try again. Each contestant that looks good to the program people gets a thorough quizzing on the chosen subject before being accepted. That's to find out if they're really experts. How are you going to handle it?"

Rick hadn't known about that. He pondered for a moment. "That means we'd have to prepare a hidden transmitter, too, so we could help out during the examination. It could be done. The contestants could wear the gadget strapped to their legs, under their skirts or trousers."

Steve was enjoying Rick's ready responses. His eyes twinkled. "You'd have to use very limited range on your Megabuck Mob transmitter, and a very high frequency. Otherwise, the Federal Communications Commission would pick you up, use a direction finder, and move in on your operation. They might locate you, anyway, even on low power and ultra-high frequency. How are you going to lick that?"

Rick held up his hands in surrender. "I'm not. I can't take a chance of getting the federal government into the act. Gosh, I'd have the FCC, the FBI, and maybe a dozen others on my trail. I quit. The Megabuck Mob is hereby dissolved."

Steve looked disappointed. "And I was hoping your plan was foolproof. I was about to buy stock in the Mob." The amusement in his eyes belied the words.

Hartson Brant laughed. "I'm glad you're the one that stuck a pin in his bubble, Steve. The way Barby bakes cakes, I'm not sure Rick could ever break one to get the file out."

Steve chuckled. "The records are full of foolproof get-rich-quick schemes like this one. And the jails are full of halfway criminal geniuses, too. But don't overlook the advantages of an eat-proof cake. It might come in handy to throw at the guards during the getaway."

The young people laughed, too, then Barby sobered suddenly. "Rick, could you really put one of those things in my hair?"

He had an image of the gadget in his mind, and he knew it would work. "Sure, Sis. Why?"

"An idea I want to talk to you about later." She turned to Steve and asked anxiously, "You do know Rick was only fooling, don't you, Steve? He wouldn't steal anything from anyone, honestly."

Steve nodded. "I do, Barby. I won't throw him in jail this time. I might need him."

"Is that what you're here for?" she asked.

"I need you all," Steve said. He motioned to chairs. "Let's sit down. Can Mrs. Brant join us?"

Hartson Brant went to get her while the young people started to deluge Steve with questions. He held up a hand in protest. "Wait until the whole family's here, please."

In a moment Mrs. Brant had joined them and greeted Steve cordially. Then the young agent got serious.

"I was only partly joking when I said I wanted to take over Spindrift. I really do, in a way. Here's why. We've had a team of scientists working on a project that's of the greatest importance to national defense.

There were four in the team, all topnotchers. Hartson, I'm sure you'll know some, if not all of them, by reputation."

Steve removed the ammunition clip from his submachine gun and sighted through the barrel, then let the bolt ram home with a sharp click. "It was my job to guard the project. As you know, I had to go to the Virgin Islands, but I left one of my best men in charge, and he did his job thoroughly. I'm satisfied about that. No unknown person has been near the project office. And no unknowns have been in close contact with any of the team. Yet, two of them are in the hospital."

"Sick or wounded?" Scotty asked.

"Neither, really. We don't know what's wrong. Their minds suddenly ceased to function."

Hartson Brant leaned forward. "You mean they're unconscious?"

Steve shook his head. "Not in the usual sense. It's as though all their thoughts and memories had suddenly been scrambled. Did you ever see a teletype machine in operation, particularly one that suddenly went haywire?"

Rick had. "The news machine did that over at the Whiteside *Morning Record*. It was typing out clear copy, then suddenly there wasn't anything but gibberish."

"That's it," Steve agreed. "And it's the best analogy I can think of for what happened to the two scientists. When a teletype goes haywire, one moment everything is clear and perfect, the next everything is scrambled. All the letters are there but they no longer make words. The scientists talk words—common, everyday words—but the words don't make thoughts or sentences. Just sounds."

"How awful," Mrs. Brant murmured. Barby looked horrified.

Rick searched his memory for anything similar he had ever read about or heard of, but there was nothing. From the expressions on their faces, his father and Scotty were equally puzzled.

"Well, even though I have absolutely no evidence of foul play, I decided not to take chances," Steve went on. "I got one of the scientists to go along with my plan. He shares my concern, simply on the basis that no known disease would affect human beings in this way, and two scientists of the same team being stricken with an unknown ailment is too much coincidence."

"He's wise," Hartson Brant agreed.

"He also has a family. The other scientist does not. He's a crusty old bachelor who thinks the whole thing is nonsense and insists on staying right where he is."

"How do we fit in?" Scotty asked. "You said you needed all of us."

"That's right. I want to relocate the project at Spindrift."

"Using the co-operative scientist as the basis for a new staff?" Rick inquired.

"Yes. We went through some of the most complicated maneuvers you ever saw to get him out of Washington with his family. I'm certain his movements cannot be traced. So his presence here will be a complete secret. But it isn't just the scientist. I'm also asking you to take in his family, consisting of his wife and daughter."

"Of course we will," Mrs. Brant said warmly.

Steve turned to Barby. "I think you'll enjoy it, because the girl is just your age, and she's a very friendly and pleasant young lady."

Barby looked pleased and excited. "What's her name?"

"Janice. Janice Miller."

"Is the scientist Dr. Walter Miller by any chance?" Hartson Brant asked quickly.

"Exactly right. Do you know him?"

"Not personally. We've never met, but a few years ago we carried on a very extensive correspondence on the subject of energy levels in nuclear isomers."

Steve grinned. "I won't pretend to know what you're talking about. But I'm glad you'll have something in common. Will you and your staff join him to make up a new project team?"

"I think we can," Hartson Brant said thoughtfully. "Some of us can put aside what we're doing. I'll have to know a little more about the project, of course."

The federal agent nodded. "Dr. Miller can give you the details personally."

Rick expressed a thought that had been on his mind. "We're sort of isolated here, but we're certainly not cut off from the world. Our friends visit us, and we go to the mainland almost every day. How do we explain who these people are? I'm sure you don't want their names to get out."

"I'll give you a cover story. Their name is Morrison. You met them through Dr. Ernst while you were in the Virgin Islands. They were very hospitable, and you're simply returning their hospitality. They know the Islands well from vacations spent there, so no one will trip them up on details."

"How about details of our trip?" Scotty asked.

"They've been briefed thoroughly, by me. You can check them and fill in any missing details."

Barby giggled. "I'm glad that you didn't have any doubts about our taking them in, Steve."

"Steve knows we're available any time he needs us, and for anything we can give," Rick said.

Steve smiled his thanks. "Well, now you can guess why I showed up with a hunk of artillery under my wing. I had to be sure there wasn't a reception party waiting. You never can tell about information leaks, no matter how careful you are, so I landed at the back end of the island with a squad of men and we went over the place with a fine-tooth comb. I didn't walk in until I was certain there wasn't a stranger on the island—including strangers you might not have known about."

THE INVASION OF SPINDRIFT 19

Hartson Brant rose. "Well, I think we've settled all initial details except where we put the Millers—or rather, the Morrisons. Can you bring them tomorrow?"

Steve rose, too. "As Rick and Barby said, I didn't have any doubts. How about tonight?"

"Tonight!" Barby gasped. "Are they here?"

"Almost. They're on a cutter offshore. If it isn't convenient, I can keep them overnight."

"Of course it's convenient," Mrs. Brant said firmly. "We'll put Mr. and Mrs. Morrison in John Gordon's room. He's still out West. And we'll take the spare twin bed out of Hobart Zircon's room and put Janice in with Barby. Bring them ashore right away, Steve. Barby and I will get busy, and Rick and Scotty can move the spare bed."

"Wonderful." Steve walked out to the porch and coughed twice. Rick hurried to his side just in time to see one of the trees in the orchard yield up a dark shadow that turned out to be a Coast Guard petty officer, carbine at the ready and a walkie-talkie slung over his shoulder.

"Let me have your horn, Smitty," Steve requested.

The coastguardman gave Rick a curious look as he handed Steve the phone.

The agent said, "Nevada, this is Texas. Deliver the goods."

The reply was, "Texas, this is Nevada. The package is in the mail."

Steve handed the phone back to the coastguardman and ordered, "Get the boys together and return to the ship, Smitty. Repeat their instructions. They don't know where they've been, and they don't know what they've been doing."

Smitty grinned. "Aye-aye, sir. That won't be hard. None of us really know where we've been or what we've been doing."

"Life is easier that way," Steve said. "Shove off, now."

"Aye-aye, sir." The guardsman faded off into the night.

"Let's move furniture," Steve suggested.

For the next few moments the house was a flurry of activity. Rick and Scotty dismantled the twin bed in Zircon's room, explaining only to the big scientist that unexpected company had arrived. Zircon, engrossed in a theoretical problem, scarcely noticed.

By the time Mrs. Brant was satisfied with arrangements and had counted the towels for the third time, Steve called from downstairs that the boat was arriving.

Rick, Scotty, and Barby ran to Steve's side and walked with him toward the landing where the Spindrift boats were moored. Dismal had paid little attention to the proceedings, but now, fearful of being left behind, the pup raced ahead of the group.

The boat carrying the Morrisons—for so Rick was already conditioning himself to think of them—was

The coastguardman gave Rick a curious look

22 THE ELECTRONIC MIND READER

approaching the dock. As the group hurried to meet the unexpected guests, two coastguardmen leaped from the big motor whaleboat and made it fast.

Dismal got there first. He barked furiously, trying to frighten off the invaders, then his barks suddenly changed to an anguished howl as a new voice joined in the racket. It was a feline voice, and a highly indignant one.

"Great grandma's ghost!" Steve exclaimed. "I forgot to tell you they have a cat!"

Dismal shot by them, followed by an enormous creature with glowing eyes that yowled at the top of its lungs, in what was probably very coarse language to anyone who spoke cat talk. Dismal had at last met his match, and was beating an inglorious retreat.

Just as Rick was about to take up the chase and rescue his pup, the cat decided to break off the engagement. The ruffled fur subsided slightly as the animal turned from the chase and approached the four who had been hurrying to the pier. In the beam of Steve's flashlight Rick saw that the cat was a huge blue Persian, and though he knew little about cats, he recognized that this was an aristocrat of its kind.

The Persian gave a meow of greeting, then walked up and rubbed against Barby's legs. It gave out a noise that reminded Rick of a wood rasp rubbing over a piece of broken pine. The cat was purring!

Barby had stamped her foot angrily at the sight of

Dismal being forced to retreat to the house, but the cat was too much for her. "You beautiful thing!" she exclaimed, and picked the creature up. It responded by purring louder.

Rick grinned. On the pet level, at least, the Morrison invasion was off to a fast start. He hoped the incident wasn't symbolic.

CHAPTER III

A System Within a System

WHEN Rick came down to breakfast the next morning, the day was already hours old for his father, Steve Ames, Julius Weiss, Parnell Winston, and Dr. Walter Miller alias Morrison. The scientists had been closeted in the library with Steve since dawn, their talks interrupted only by Mrs. Brant serving coffee to the group. Steve, too, had remained overnight.

Barby and Scotty were around the island somewhere with Janice. Mrs. Brant and Mrs. Morrison were in the kitchen, getting acquainted and finding that they had friends in common.

It wasn't that Rick had slept late; he was on time. Everyone else had gotten up early. Rick told himself that he was the only calm member of the family, but underneath he was a little chagrined. If he had arisen earlier, he might have been able to take part in the talks now going on in the library.

The Morrisons had been so tired from the strain of

getting out of Washington undetected, and from the trip in the confined quarters of the Coast Guard cutter that they had gone to bed almost immediately.

Dr. Morrison turned out to be a tall man with a kind, tired face, steel-rimmed glasses, and a shock of curly white hair. Mrs. Morrison was a pleasant, stylish woman whose reaction was a mixture of pure pleasure at finding herself in the comfortable Brant home and embarrassment at the circumstances that had forced her to impose herself on strangers. Rick had liked both the Morrisons immediately.

His reaction to Janice was favorable, too. He admitted that she was a remarkably pretty girl, as dark as Barby was fair, and of about the same height and slimness. She hadn't said a great deal, and he decided at once that she was shy. Barby had taken to her immediately, and she to Barby. The last thing Rick had heard before falling asleep was the two of them talking and giggling in the room down the hall.

He walked into the dining room, hoping he wasn't too late for breakfast, and stopped short, stifling a laugh at the sight that met his eyes.

The Morrisons' cat, whose name was Shah, was crouched on one of the dining-room chairs. Dismal was sniffing around beneath the chair, obviously looking for the cat. As Rick watched, Dismal gave up the search and walked from under the chair. Instantly he was batted on the nose from above by a paw that moved with supersonic speed. Rick laughed as Dismal gave a cry of pure frustration and headed for the kitchen at a trot. The cat had been playing, since the blow was struck with claws sheathed. If Shah had wanted to hurt the pup, raking claws could have torn deep furrows.

Rick stroked the silky fur and Shah purred hoarsely. He hadn't had much experience with cats, but he liked this one. The Persian had a sense of humor. Rick went into the kitchen and consoled Dismal, after bidding good morning to his mother and Mrs. Morrison. The pup rolled over on his back and played dead, his only trick. The boy scratched Dismal's stomach until the pup's hind leg flailed in delighted ecstasy.

"Am I too late for breakfast?" Rick asked his mother.

"Of course not. We'll be ready in ten minutes."

Rick wandered out to the screened front porch that was the Brants' summer living room. The ocean was calm this morning. He searched the horizon for some sign of the Coast Guard cutter. There was none, which didn't surprise him. Steve was too old a hand to attract attention to Spindrift by having a government craft waiting offshore.

Barby, Jan, and Scotty were walking from the long, low gray laboratory building on the southeast corner of the island, past the place where the Sky Wagon, his plane, usually was staked down. His landing strip ran along the seaward edge of the island, from the lab building to the front of the house. However, the plane still carried the pontoons with which it had been fitted for the Virgin Islands trip, and for the time being, it was drawn ashore at Pirate's Field.

Presently the trio joined him on the porch. Jan smiled and said good morning in her soft voice. Scotty said, "I thought you were going to sleep all day."

Barby came to Rick's defense. "He was tired. After all, it's hard work to get wonderful ideas like the one he had last night."

Apparently Barby had told Jan all about it, because the girl asked, "Can I be a member of the Megabuck Mob?" There seemed to be just a touch of wistfulness about the way she added, "You always seem to be having adventures of one sort or another at Spindrift."

Rick answered, "Please don't believe everything Barby tells you. She exaggerates, sort of."

"I do not," Barby answered emphatically. "We do have adventures. Besides, Jan already knew about some of them, because she read about Spindrift in the papers. And she's already a member of the Mob, because I invited her!"

Rick interpreted Barby's glare correctly. It said that if he wasn't gracious and nice to their new guest, he would have his sister to reckon with, and, as he knew full well, she was no mean adversary.

"Fine," he said. "Welcome to the Mob, Miss Morrison. We'll assign you the subject of economic history."

"Jan, please," she answered, then smiled shyly. "But couldn't I have another subject? I'm just not the type to know much about economics, I guess."

"That's just the point," Scotty explained.

Barby had a serious look on her pert face. "Of course Rick's idea about stealing a million from quiz shows was just a joke. But, Rick, you gave me an idea—if you'll co-operate."

"It depends on the idea," Rick answered warily.

"Oh, don't be so cautious. I'm not trying to trap you into taking me on any trips." Barby referred to the promise she had once wangled out of her brother that she could go on the next expedition, a promise that had gotten the Spindrift young people entangled in a hazardous adventure in the far-off South Seas.

Rick perched on the arm of a sofa. "Okay. Let's have it."

"Well, I was thinking about the Harvest Moon Show at school." She explained, in an aside to Jan, "Every October the high school puts on a big variety show in the city auditorium to raise money for the school athletic fund. Rick said he could make me a radio receiver that I could wear in my hair."

"He can," Scotty interjected. "Remember the control radios we made for the Tractosaur? He could make one for you the same way."

The Tractosaur was a "thinking bulldozer" the Spindrift scientists had designed.

Barby continued, "I know you can make a small

A SYSTEM WITHIN A SYSTEM

transmitter that will fit in your pocket, because that's all the Tractosaur control was, really. Well, if I wore a receiver that no one could see, and if you carried a transmitter that no one could see, we could put on the most wonderful mind-reading act in history!"

Rick's quick imagination elaborated on Barby's words. It was a great idea! He could work among the audience, while Barby sat blindfolded on the stage. He would choose a person in the audience and ask for something from wallet or purse, and whisper: "Please let me have your driver's license. Thank you. Mr. Charles Rogers, is it? . . . Where is 3218 Newark Drive? . . . Oh, over by the airfield. Well, Mr. Rogers, let me see if I can transmit all this information telepathically to my sister." Then he would hold up the driver's license and say loudly, "What have I here?" And Barby, who had heard every whispered word, would answer. He would coax the information out of her, and the audience would be baffled.

"Sensational," he complimented her. "We'll do it."

"Brant and Brant," Scotty intoned, "the marvels of the universe! See the living proof of the science of parapsychology! Mystifying, terrifying, a scientific phenomenon without parallel that has baffled the leading minds of the world!" Scotty's quick mind also had caught the implications of Barby's idea.

Jan Morrison was a scientist's daughter, too, and printed electronic circuits were no mystery to her. She said enthusiastically, "You could even do mind reading at a distance."

"How?" Barby asked.

"Well, if there were two transmitters, Scotty could have one, too. He could go to someone outside the auditorium, like the mayor, or some other official, and have him write a sentence on a sheet of paper, which Scotty could read over his shoulder. Then Barby, on the auditorium stage, would ask everyone to look at their watches, and say that the mayor had just written so and so on a sheet of paper, then burned it. Scotty would bring the mayor to the auditorium, and Barby would tell him what she had said, and at what time, and ask him if it was right. Of course it would be."

Rick looked at the girl with new respect. It was a very good gimmick indeed. He said as much.

Barby put her arm around Jan's waist. "We'll be sure to invite you to the show. Won't it be fun?"

"If it's safe for us to let people know where we are by then," Jan said somberly.

They fell silent at the reminder that Jan's presence was far more serious than a casual visit. Finally Rick said, "We'll get to work on the sets this afternoon."

"Make it tomorrow," Barby said quickly. "I sort of promised Jan something . . ."

Rick and Scotty exchanged glances.

"I said you and Scotty would teach her how to use the aqualungs."

Rick breathed a sigh of relief. That would be no hardship. He and Scotty needed practice, anyway.

A SYSTEM WITHIN A SYSTEM

They had hardly used the lungs since returning from the Virgin Islands.

Mrs. Brant summoned them to breakfast and they walked in to find Steve and the scientists gathered at the big table.

"Got everything settled?" Rick asked.

"Just about," Steve replied. "We have a job for you, though."

Rick's pulse quickened. "What is it?"

"Your father and Weiss will need to pay a quick trip to Washington. I want you to take them in the Sky Wagon."

"When?" Scotty inquired.

"Tomorrow morning. You'll come back tomorrow afternoon."

Over breakfast, Rick tried to get more information from the agent. "Exactly what are we working on, Steve?"

Ames sipped steaming coffee thoughtfully. "Ever hear of a weapon system?"

Rick had. "It's a weapon so complicated, with so many parts, that it's actually a system instead of just a simple weapon. I think the term is used mostly for missiles."

"You think right. Well, Winston, Weiss, and your father will help Dr. Morrison do the basic design work on a system to go into a weapon system."

Scotty had been listening, too. "How complicated can you get?" he asked.

Dr. Morrison answered. "When it comes to missile

work, you can get fantastically complicated. In fact, some missile systems are so complicated it's a wonder they ever work at all."

The telephone rang. Barby, who served when necessary as the island's switchboard operator, ran to answer. In a moment she returned. "It's for you, Steve. From Washington. I plugged it in on the library extension."

Steve excused himself. A few moments later he returned. "Hartson, I just took the liberty of ordering a scrambler placed on your phone switchboard, in case we need to hold any classified conversations between here and my offices. The phone man will install it today, if you have no objection."

"Of course not," Hartson Brant said. "I think it's a sensible precaution, especially with one member of the team remaining in Washington."

"What's a scrambler?" Barby asked.

"A special device that turns phone conversations into jumbled gibberish so no one can understand them. You talk normally, and sound normal to the person listening. But anyone tapping in on the line gets only sounds that mean nothing."

The agent's face turned grim. "Speaking of gibberish reminds me of the reason for the call. The *Washington Post* carried a story in one of its columns this morning hinting that two scientists working on a supersecret project had been driven insane. It also hinted that the insanity was an effect of the gadget they were working on!"

CHAPTER IV

A Haircut and a Wink

Rick held the Sky Wagon at the altitude to which he had been assigned by the control tower at Anacostia Naval Air Station in Washington. He was a little nervous because there was more air traffic around him than he had ever seen before.

Across the Potomac River, so close that the traffic patterns almost interlocked, was busy Washington National Airport. Below him along the Anacostia River were two military airports; Anacostia, at which he would land, and Bolling Air Force Base. And to complicate matters slightly, Andrews Air Force Base was only a short distance away.

A thousand feet above his head a tremendous Air Force Stratocruiser circled patiently. A thousand feet below him a flight of Navy Banshee fighters awaited clearance for landing. And climbing through the pattern came a division of Air Force F-80's.

Rick's neck ached from swiveling around. Scotty

was helping him watch for other aircraft. But in the rear seat, Hartson Brant and Julius Weiss talked a steady stream, as they had ever since taking off from Spindrift. Rick wished he were as oblivious to the traffic. Actually, he didn't know what they were talking about. Good as his scientific training was, they were in a realm where his young mind hadn't even probed.

His earphones gave out: "Tower to Spindrift Flight. You are cleared to land. Approach from Northeast."

Rick glanced down in time to see the Navy fighters peel off in a precision maneuver that was lovely to watch. Then, on their heels, he stood the Sky Wagon up on a wing and slid down toward the muddy river below.

A short time later Rick called for instructions and was told to beach at Ramp Three. He located it without difficulty. Scotty climbed out on the pontoon and caught the rope thrown by a seaman. In a few moments they were beached.

A stocky young man who might have been a government clerk approached and introduced himself as Tom Dodd. The identification folder he held out bore the familiar JANIG imprint. "Steve phoned ahead," he said. "Do you need anything for your plane?"

"We'd better top off the tank," Rick said. "Everything else is all right." He described the kind of gas his plane used, fearful that the Navy might use either a higher or lower octane that would not be suitable.

Dodd gave instructions to a Navy petty officer, then led the Spindrifters to a waiting sedan. Rick got into the back seat and slumped back between his father and Weiss. The little mathematician looked at him in some alarm.

"Rick! You look done in. What on earth is wrong?"

He smiled feebly. "I'm a sissy, Professor. The only other times I've flown into Washington I landed at light-plane airports outside the city. This morning I got right into the middle of the big kids. Honest, the traffic was worse than Times Square. I was so scared I'd lose position and bang into someone that I almost swiveled my head off."

Tom Dodd looked back and grinned sympathetically. "Don't feel badly. Even the commercial pilots sit up straight and keep bright-eyed on the Washington approach. Airwise, it's one of the most crowded cities in the world."

As Tom steered the big sedan expertly through the traffic en route to downtown Washington, Rick asked his father, "What were you and Professor Weiss talking about? You lost me just about the time we got air-borne."

The scientist shook his head. "This time, Rick, I can't help much. Ask me again when you've completed your undergraduate work in college."

"I'm afraid your father is right," Weiss agreed. "When one gets deeply into the physical sciences there are no longer simple mechanical analogies; there are only equations that I'm afraid are beyond you for now, Rick."

Rick sighed. "A lot of help I'm going to be on this project!"

"You're not supposed to help," his father corrected. "The project is entirely for the purpose of developing principles for the system. The final product will be the equations with which the technologists can begin actual system design. In other words, we are working only on the first theoretical step."

"But the newspaper article said the scientists were affected by a gadget," Scotty objected.

"The article was wrong. Paper covered with mathematical computations can scarcely affect anyone," Hartson Brant said decisively.

Rick stared through the window. The sedan was moving down Constitution Avenue toward 14th Street. "But how did the newspaper find out anything in the first place?"

Dodd swung the sedan around a truck, then shrugged expressively. "We'd like to know. Columnists have their sources of information. Usually the source isn't close to the inside dope, so most of the columns are pretty inaccurate. A good thing, too, otherwise the enemy would be getting our top-secret information in print all the time. Probably this leak came from someone in the hospital where the team members were taken."

Conversation lapsed until Dodd swung the sedan

into a restricted parking place near the corner of 15th and K streets. Then he led the way into an office building. Rick looked around him as they walked to the elevators. It was a typical large office building with an arcade-type lobby. He noticed a haberdashery shop, a barbershop, a florist, a newspaper-tobacco stand, and the entrance to a drug store. The building directory was loaded with names.

In the elevator, Dodd said, "Four, please."

The Spindrifters were the only ones that got off at that floor. As the door slid closed, Rick saw that a man was seated in an alcove, just out of sight of anyone who got off the elevator. Dodd greeted him, then said, "Remember these faces, Sam."

Sam nodded without speaking.

Dodd led them down a hall. Rick had to satisfy his curiosity. "Is this a government building?"

"No. It's a regular office building. We leased this floor under the name of a phony corporation. It's entirely ours, but the rest of the building is occupied by legitimate firms."

"Isn't that risky?" Weiss asked.

"It depends. If the project is penetrated, then it becomes easier for the enemy in one way, since we don't have the protection of a government building. On the other hand, the public has free access to all but a few of the government buildings, while we can control who comes in and out of this floor."

"What does 'penetrated' mean?" Scotty inquired.

"Known to the enemy."

"But couldn't you have put the project in the Pentagon, or in the Atomic Energy Commission Building?" Rick pursued.

"Yes, except that it's top secret, even within the government. I doubt that more than two dozen people even know about it. Remember, the best security is not to let people even suspect that a thing exists."

"But the project has been penetrated," Scotty pointed out.

"We don't know that. The newspaper article gave no details, remember. Only that some unidentified scientists had gone insane. No location, no names, no anything of real value. And we have taken precautions. After all, you have the team chief. Only one man is left, and we hope to get him out of here, too."

Dodd swung open a door that opened into a bare outer office, and led them into an inner room where a man bent over a desk.

Rick knew his name. This was Dr. Humphrey Marks, the reluctant bachelor. All Rick could see for the moment was a bald head. It was completely bald, not even a fringe of hair remaining. It gleamed in the light of the desk lamp. Presently the bald pate revolved back and a truculent face stared up at them.

Dr. Marks looked like a man who had been born impatient. His underslung jaw thrust forward as he demanded, "Well, well? What is this, Dodd? Well? Who are these people?"

Dodd was unperturbed. "Dr. Brant, Dr. Weiss, and Richard Brant and Donald Scott."

Marks harrumphed. He stood erect, and he was scarcely taller than little Julius Weiss. He had a solid, square build and massive hands. "I am honored, gentlemen," he said crisply. "Sit down."

The Spindrifters did so. "We will get to business," Marks stated. "You will forgive me if I begin on an elementary level. It is only for the purpose of defining the problem. Ames said you had been briefed by Miller, so I will confine the briefing to my part of the project."

Hartson Brant and Julius Weiss produced notebooks. Rick and Scotty relaxed as best they could in the uncomfortable chairs and prepared to listen.

"You are, of course, aware of the problems inherent in the development of inertial systems," Marks began. "Perturbations are many, and both predictable and random. Consider our missile. We set its little brain for a given pattern. We depend on its inertia to inform the brain when perturbations are pulling it off course. The brain then takes the necessary corrective action. This, of course, is oversimplification."

It wasn't very simple to Rick. He squirmed uncomfortably on the hard chair.

"Now, we have dealt primarily with the perturbations one would expect. The equatorial bulge, for example. The result? We still have a probable error of several miles in hitting the target. This is not to be borne, gentlemen. We must have precision. Now, what information do we have that allows such precision? We have the effects of perturbation of the other planetary bodies and of the sun itself. These we may calculate closely. We shall use them to guide our missile, as they interact with the missile's own inertia."

Marks broke off to glare at Rick. He inquired acidly, "Do I perhaps bore you? Or have you a serious itch? If so, scratch it, for heaven's sake. You are squirming so, I can see only a blur through the corner of my eye."

Hartson Brant came to his son's rescue. He looked at Dodd. "May the boys be excused? I'm sure this discussion will be of no value to them, and probably they have some things they would like to do."

Dodd nodded. "If you decide to leave the vicinity, let Sam know."

"We'll be in the lobby," Rick said. He motioned to Scotty. His feelings were of mixed relief at getting out of there and irritation at Marks for what amounted to summary dismissal.

As they walked to the elevator, Rick asked, "What did you make out of that?"

"Not much. How about you?"

"A little," Rick admitted. "Enough to know what the project is aiming at."

"Which is?"

"A guidance system for the intercontinental missile, and a fantastic one that uses the moon and

A HAIRCUT AND A WINK 41

the sun, and maybe Venus and Mars as guideposts."

Scotty whistled. "As you said, a lot of good we'll be to this project. Well, what do we do now?"

Rick ran a hand through his hair. "Follow Barby's instructions." His sister had said bluntly that both he and Scotty were getting as shaggy as Dismal, and please get haircuts. He knew why, of course. Barby wanted them to be at their best, because she liked Jan Morrison very much and wanted Jan to like the boys, too.

Sam nodded to them as they walked to the elevator. Rick noted that the guard could watch the stairs as well as the elevator doors. He also noted that the guard's coat was loose, and that the butt of a Magnum revolver was within easy reach of his hand. Knowing how Steve Ames operated, Rick also suspected that other, less visible, methods had been taken to guard the fourth floor, but there was nothing he could see.

It was still early in the day and the barbershop in the lobby was not crowded. Rick and Scotty both were able to get chairs.

Rick browsed through a magazine as the barber worked, but found nothing of interest. He put it down and looked around him. The shop was like any other shop, anywhere. He thought that barbershops may vary in the number of chairs, the luxuriousness of the appointments, and the size of the mirrors, but they all have about the same smell, and the same collection of bottles for the barber's use.

However, one item attracted Rick's attention, because it seemed out of place. It looked for all the world like the hair driers one finds in beauty shops. There was a stand, and a metal hood.

He gestured toward it. "What's that?"

"It's for treating dry hair," the barber answered. "Special oil treatment, with electric massage. Very good."

Rick's hair was dry from frequent immersion in both salt and fresh water. Being inquisitive about everything in the world, he thought about trying it.

"Maybe I'll have time for a treatment," he said.

The barber ran a hand through the boy's light-brown hair. "You don't need one. Your hair is healthy, and not especially dry. I wouldn't give you a treatment you don't need."

"Have it your way," Rick said. The barber was either too lazy or too honest for his own good. In all probability the machine would do nothing Rick couldn't do for himself with his own two hands.

There was a good view of the elevators through the barbershop windows. Rick watched people coming and going, and speculated for his own amusement on who they might be, and their business in the building. Speculation was idle, of course. Take Tom Dodd. No one, without inside knowledge, would suspect that he was a federal agent engaged in guarding a hush-hush project on the fourth floor. Or Dr. Marks. Who would suspect that he carried a vital secret? Or, more accurately, that he was working on one?

A HAIRCUT AND A WINK 43

As the barber was brushing Rick off, the boy saw his father step out of the elevator, stop, and look around. He saw the elevator operator step from the car, look into the barbershop, and wink. Rick almost winked back, then he realized that the operator was winking at the barber and not at him.

The scientist saw Rick at almost the same moment and walked into the barbershop. "Julius will be busy for another half hour," he said. "I think I'll follow your example, Rick." He climbed into the chair Rick had just vacated.

Scotty was through, too. The boys took seats and busied themselves reading magazines.

Hartson Brant's hair had needed only trimming, not complete cutting, so he was finished in a short time. The barber shook out his cloth, then put it back on for the finishing touches. Rick glanced up as the barber spoke.

"Your hair's pretty dry, sir, and I have an excellent treatment here. I'd like to give you one. It would make your hair look better, and make it easier to handle."

Tension swept through Rick as though someone had turned on an electric current. The tension had no focus. It was just that something deep within him had reacted. He stood up and dropped his magazine.

"Dad," he said hastily, "I just saw Julius go through the lobby."

"Where did he go?" Hartson Brant demanded. "I didn't see him."

"I think he went through the front door," Rick said. "Better hurry. I'll try to catch him."

Outside the barbershop he stopped, to let Scotty catch up with him. "Why should Weiss run out through the front door?" Scotty demanded.

"He didn't. It was a stall, to get Dad out of there in a hurry."

"But why?"

"I don't know," Rick said slowly. "For some reason, I just didn't want him to have that dry-hair treatment!"

CHAPTER V

JANIG Runs a Security Check

THERE wasn't much evidence on which to base his reaction, Rick admitted. But when he reacted, he just reacted and that's all there was to it. Call it a hunch, or call it nonsense. That's how it was, and he couldn't change it.

The barber had practically refused him a dry-hair treatment—and his hair was rather dry. The same barber had tried to sell a treatment to Hartson Brant —whose hair was not dry at all. And the elevator boy who had carried the scientist down from the fourth floor had winked at the barber.

Even admitting that it added up to no evidence of anything, it bothered him. He had asked Tom Dodd how much JANIG knew about the barber.

Tom admitted that JANIG didn't know much. After all, he pointed out, it was impossible to check everyone in an office building of that size, or at least impractical. Furthermore, it was a cover operation, and any kind of a careful check on people in the building would warn them that something was going on. Tom agreed, however, that it was better to be safe than sorry. JANIG would run a check on the barber, even though Rick's evidence was no evidence at all.

Rick wasn't satisfied. He felt he had to talk it over with Steve Ames, and called the agent, who was in JANIG's New York office, as soon as he got home.

There was a small switch box next to the telephone in the library. It had only two positions, one marked "normal" and the other not marked at all.

Steve asked, "Who is it?"

"Rick."

"Throw your switch."

Rick did so, with no apparent results. "Nothing happened," he said.

"Nothing audible," Steve corrected. "I threw mine at the same time. We're scrambled. Go ahead, Rick, what is it?"

Rick told him the story. Steve didn't laugh. He had had experience with Rick's hunches before. "All right. I've already talked with Tom Dodd. He told me the story and I agreed we should run a check. He also reported that Weiss had persuaded Marks to come to Spindrift so the team could work together. I have Dodd planning how to get him out of Washington."

"Tom told me why no check had been run on the

people in the building," Rick said hesitantly. "Honestly, Steve, I thought you always checked on everyone who might have a connection with a case."

"We do," Steve said flatly. "But we can't check on everyone in the city of Washington. Consider, Rick. There are several hundred people that work in the building and perhaps as many more who go there regularly for perfectly legitimate reasons. We couldn't run a deep check on all of them, and a superficial check wouldn't mean anything. So we don't check. Instead, we make sure we know about the people the scientists see regularly, and we give physical protection not only to the scientists but to the floor they work on. We keep a careful check to be sure our phones aren't tapped, and there's a scrambler on each line. Of course the moment we get even a slight odor of fish, we run a check. That's why we're working on your barber right now. We're also checking the elevator operator."

"All right. I was off base, I guess."

"Not at all. I'd be disappointed if you didn't ask for explanations."

There was one other question in Rick's mind. "How do you know we weren't followed back to Spindrift?"

Steve chuckled. "You had two cars on your tail. They'd have picked up anyone who tried to follow Tom. What's more, our men at the airport identified every plane that took off from the vicinity of Washington for two hours after your departure."

Rick said sheepishly, "Sorry, Steve."

"Forget it. I'll be in touch with you, Rick."

Steve was right, of course. JANIG was on the job and would plug any loose holes. And once Marks arrived, Spindrift would be the only base the JANIG men had to cover. That would make it simpler. Rick decided he might as well put the matter out of his mind.

Barby, Jan, and Scotty were waiting for him on the front porch.

Scotty asked, "What gives?"

"Steve says to forget it."

Jan frowned, her pretty face worried. "Barby told me about these odd hunches you sometimes get. Aren't they ever wrong?"

Rick grinned. "I'll say they are. Don't worry, Jan. You're safe here."

Her dark eyes flashed at him. "I'm not worried about myself. I'm worried about my father."

Rick apologized. "I didn't mean that quite the way it sounded. But don't forget, Jan. Our father is in this, too. So we'll worry with you—if there's any worrying to be done."

Barby changed the subject. "It's still early. Why can't we give Jan another swimming lesson?"

They had started the day before teaching Jan how to use underwater breathing apparatus. She was an excellent swimmer, almost as good as Barby. But she had never had experience with mask, fins, and snorkel, so lessons in the use of those were required before she could graduate to the aqualungs.

"Let's go," Rick said.

In a short time the four had changed to swimming suits and were testing the water off Pirate's Beach. It was cold, but not unbearable. Once they were accustomed to it, Rick picked up the instructions where he had left off the day before. Jan was using Barby's mask, snorkel, and fins. They would get her some of her own on the first trip to Whiteside.

Barby had borrowed her father's equipment. The mask wasn't a perfect fit, but she was experienced enough not to mind a little leakage. The snorkel was all right, since no fit was involved, but the fins were ludicrous on her small feet. She had stuffed cotton in the toes to make them tight enough to wear, but that made the fins hard to control.

"Follow the leader!" Rick called. "I'll lead, Jan next, Scotty next, and Barby bring up the rear."

That was so Scotty would be instantly aware of any trouble Jan got into. Barby could swim as well as either of the boys and needed no watching.

Rick started by going straight out, watching the bottom through his mask. When he got to about the fifteen-foot depth, he bent at the waist and threw his legs upward. He slid smoothly into the water, rolling on his back to watch Jan. She imitated his movements perfectly, and he turned back, satisfied. She was graceful as a seal in the water. It wouldn't take much to make a first-class diver out of her.

Rick went to the bottom and moved along, doing underwater acrobatics and touching a rock here and there. Then he turned over on his back again and started upward, eyes on Jan. She followed. He led the way back to the beach.

As the group emerged from the water and lifted their masks, Rick looked at Scotty. His pal nodded. "She'll do. She followed you like a shadow."

"Good. All right, Jan. Next step is clearing your mask of water. The principle is easy. Just remember that gas is lighter than liquid. Your breath is lighter than the water. So you hold the top of your mask and blow it full of air, which forces the water out the bottom. Watch."

He demonstrated a few times, then Jan tried it. She caught on easily.

The instruction continued, until at the end of two hours, Rick took all of Jan's equipment and threw it into twelve feet of water. "Now," he said calmly, "go after it and put it on in the water. Clear your mask and snorkel, then come back to shore with full gear on and operating. No surfacing to take a breath. Use only the snorkel."

Jan looked into the water thoughtfully. The moments ticked by. Finally Rick asked, "What is it?"

The girl smiled. "I'm planning how I'll do it. If I don't plan in advance, it will be too late after I've started, and I intend to do it right the first time."

Rick, Barby, and Scotty exclaimed together,

"Good girl!" They laughed, and Rick explained, "That's what makes a safe diver. Know what you're going to do before you have to do it."

Jan filled her lungs and dove. The three swam out over her and watched through their masks. She found the mask, and there was a bad moment when she got it on upside down, but she quickly reversed it, held it to her face, and blew it clear. Only then did she bother with the strap that held it.

Rick watched, pleased. He hadn't told her it wasn't necessary to attach the mask before clearing. She put the snorkel mouthpiece in place, but did not bother to attach the rubber strap to her head. Then, working smoothly but without waste of time, she slipped on the fins and flashed to the surface. The snorkel emerged and she blew it clear, then swam to the beach.

"Perfect," Rick applauded.

"You're a natural," Scotty added.

Barby just beamed.

Jan was obviously pleased at their praise, but she was a little shy, too, so she contented herself with smiling her thanks.

"Aqualung instruction tomorrow morning," Rick said. "Come on. I've worked up an appetite."

That evening Rick began work on the radio circuits, as he had promised Barby. The transmitters would be the easiest part, since he could use the same circuits that had gone into the design of the Tractosaur controls, modified only slightly for use on the highest amateur band. Fortunately, Rick had both an operator's and station licenses as a radio "ham," so Barby's scheme wouldn't mean illegal operation.

The girls wandered into the shop where he and Scotty were at work, but there was nothing exciting about the painstaking work of laying out diagrams, so they soon left.

Scotty paused in his work of assembling the parts they would need. "Rick, how about making transceivers instead of simple transmitters?"

"So we can send and receive on the same unit? We can do it, all right. But why?"

"I was just thinking. Quite a few times we'd have been a lot better off if we could talk back and forth at a distance. There's no reason why these have to be designed just for you and Barby to use in the mind-reading act."

Scotty was right, of course. He usually was. "We'll make a pair of transceivers, and a receiver for Barby. Unless you think we ought to build a transceiver into her outfit, too."

"Would it be much work?"

"Not much. We might as well, I suppose."

They buckled down to the job. Rick found he couldn't work long, however. "I've still got that guitar-string feeling," he admitted. "I'm all tight inside." He didn't like it, and there was no apparent reason for it. But that didn't help him to get rid of it.

Scotty knew Rick from long experience. "Wish I

could help," he said, "but I'm stymied. There's nothing we can get our teeth into. Those two scientists bother me. I can't imagine what would put two perfectly sensible and healthy people into a state like Steve describes."

"Same here." Rick had thought about it a number of times in the past day, but had reached no conclusion. "But if it's from natural causes, how did Marks and Miller—I mean Morrison—escape?"

Scotty grinned wryly. "You're not asking me because you expect an answer."

"No," Rick agreed. He said abruptly, "I've had it. Let's hit the hay."

He might have felt better, or worse, had he been able to tune in on a conversation between Tom Dodd and Steve Ames that was going on at that very moment.

"We've had seven men on it ever since this morning," Tom was saying. "We checked him from here to breakfast, and the record is absolutely negative. Same for the elevator operator. The barber is a wanderer, never stays in one shop for long. He's hunting another job right now. The machine is his, and it's the only one of its kind. We sent Mike Malone in for a treatment. He says the machine is good. Apparently it's nothing but a hood with three massage machines installed on spring mounts, so they fit the head. The barber applies oil, then turns on the machine. It has dials, but they're fakes. It's a massage machine, pure and simple, and it passed the health inspection board, so we know it's not harmful."

Steve Ames said thoughtfully, "Negative record. Hmm. Well, at least no one has ever caught up with him if he happens to be a wrong one. It doesn't prove he's clean."

"Too true. Any ideas?"

"Just keep an eye on him. He's innocent until we get some evidence that he may be guilty. Same for the elevator operator. But, for now, we'll consider you've drawn a blank and let it go at that."

CHAPTER VI

A Calm Precedes a Storm

A CRISIS had arisen and Rick and Scotty could only stand by helplessly. After all, what could mere males do in such a situation?

Barby decided that Rick and Scotty were to fly over to Whiteside and get diving equipment for Jan, so she could have her own. It was easy to agree on the type of face mask, snorkel, and fins. But everything bogged down when it came to color.

Rick's own mask, snorkel, and fins were sea green. Scotty had a green mask, blue snorkel, and black fins. Barby had a white mask, red snorkel, and white fins.

"Look," Rick said impatiently. "What earthly difference does it make? The principal thing is comfort. If the fins feel good and the mask fits comfortably, that's it. Color? What difference does color make to a fish?"

Barby sniffed. "I wouldn't expect you to understand."

Jan looked at him coldly and stated that she wouldn't know what difference color made to a fish, because she was not a fish.

"You swim like one," Scotty said diplomatically, but didn't even get a smile in return.

There was only one thing for the boys to do, and that was to make as graceful a retreat as possible. They did so, and sat waiting under a tree in the orchard while raging debate went on between the girls on the porch.

Rick looked over at the laboratory building. His father and the other scientists were hard at work on the project, he supposed. He felt rather left out, because they were too busy to talk with him, and when he went in to look around he could see only stacks of paper covered with equations that he couldn't begin to understand.

"Wonder when Marks will arrive?" he asked.

Scotty shrugged. "We'll probably find out when he gets here."

Dr. Marks had agreed to join the team at Spindrift as soon as he finished running some of the team calculations through the automatic computer at the Bureau of Standards in Washington. Tom Dodd would arrive with him, Steve had reported. Meanwhile, protection for the Spindrift team was under the direction of another of Steve's men, Joe Blake. Joe and another agent took turns in the laboratory,

A CALM PRECEDES A STORM

sleeping and eating there and emerging one at a time for a little exercise.

Nor were Joe and his partner the only protection. In the woods on the mainland, just out of sight of the tidal flat, a group of four Boy Scout leaders were encamped, working on special camping and pioneering qualifications that would enable them to become qualified instructors for their Scout Troops. The Whiteside newspaper had even carried a brief story about the Scout activities. But Jerry Webster, Rick's friend and newspaper reporter, hadn't known when he wrote the story that the Scout leaders carried an astonishing amount of armament for such a peaceful expedition. The JANIG agents, however, had been chosen for the assignment because they really were Scout leaders in their home communities. The story would stand investigation.

Barby and Jan left the porch and walked to where the boys waited.

"We've decided," Barby announced.

The boys applauded politely.

"You see," she went on, "I'm blond, and Jan is brunette."

Rick squinted up at the girls. "By golly," he exclaimed, "that's right!" He put a hand on his heart. "One with hair filled with captured sunlight, the other with hair like the raven's wing, filled with the gleams of moonlight."

Barby threatened him with her foot. "Be serious!"

Rick composed his face in stern lines. "I am."

"Well," Barby continued, "we decided that Jan should wear a white suit and white equipment. It will make her dark hair and her tan look very dramatic. But of course I can't wear white if she does."

This was beyond Rick. Why they couldn't wear the same color was outside of his comprehension. "Of course not," he murmured politely.

"So I'm going with you. We both have to have new bathing suits, a white one for Jan and a dark-blue one for me. And I'm going to give Jan my mask and fins, because they're white. So I'll have to get blue equipment for me. And my snorkel is red, and that just won't do, because . . ."

Scotty held up his hand. "Say no more. I will swap snorkels with you, because mine is blue."

"I knew you would when you understood," Barby said smugly.

"I don't understand, but I'll trade. Come on. Let's go to Whiteside."

Jan remained behind, because Steve had not given permission for the Morrisons to leave the island, and Rick refused to take the responsibility in spite of Barby's pleading. The best he could do was to promise to call Steve about it and perhaps get permission for future trips.

The Sky Wagon landed at Whiteside pier, and the trio went to the nearby garage where the Brants' car was kept. Hartson Brant had decided it was more convenient to have a car available for use at all times than to depend on taxis, or on friends.

A CALM PRECEDES A STORM 59

The local sporting goods store had a good stock of equipment and Barby was able to purchase what she wanted without difficulty. But when it came to the bathing suits, she debated over the large selection for an hour before choosing two that were identical except for color. Rick and Scotty waited impatiently, now and then prodding Barby to hurry up. She refused to be hurried.

Back at Spindrift, Jan met them with a greeting. "That certainly didn't take long! Barby, how on earth could you pick these out so quickly?"

The boys looked at each other. Their opinion was that Barby had taken just one hour longer than necessary. Here, obviously, was that mysterious thing, the feminine mind at work. Rick examined the problem from the scientific viewpoint and got nowhere. The ways of girls defied analysis.

Both boys had to admit, however, that the results of Barby's shopping had been worth the delay. Their own rather shabby swim trunks, torn and stained from contact with undersea rocks and coral, suddenly seemed sloppy. But when Barby examined the aqualung tanks distastefully and demanded that Rick paint them to match the new suits, both boys put their feet down emphatically.

"The tanks are that color because they've been treated to withstand rust and corrosion," Rick stated. "If we paint 'em, the paint will only get knocked off and they'll look terrible. I won't do it."

The girls exchanged a glance that seemed to

say, "Boys! They have such stubborn, silly ideas!"

Jan had already gone through the exercise of clearing the aqualung hoses of water, clearing her mask while using the lung underwater, and using the reserve lever on the tank, and Rick had instructed her in the theory of diving.

Now it was time to put what she had learned to the ultimate test.

The boys hauled the equipment down to the beach in Rick's old coaster wagon, modified for carrying equipment, then directed the girls to check the regulators, check the tanks, and connect regulators to tanks preparatory to diving.

They lolled on the beach and watched. Scotty grinned. "This is the life. Tony Briotti tells me it's always this way in primitive societies. The men loaf while the women work. I'm in favor of it."

"I'm sure you are," Barby said acidly.

Jan said nothing, but continued to work with meticulous care. Rick watched closely, and was satisfied. There was ample equipment for all. Scotty helped Barby into her gear while Rick instructed Jan.

"This is the tough part. If you make it, that's the end. From then on all you'll need is practice. We'll all swim down to the fifty-foot depth. Watch your ears and don't try to continue down if you feel any pain. Go back up a few feet and try to clear your ears. When we get to the bottom, I want you to take off all your equipment, swim away from it, then swim back and put it on. Okay?"

Jan gave him a tremulous smile. "I think so."

"Good. Plan how you'll do it. Remember, air is the last thing you'll need, and the first."

"I'll remember."

It was easy enough for a diver with plenty of experience, and the confidence that experience brings, but Rick remembered from his own training that it was plenty rough the first time.

He held the tank while Jan got into harness and said reassuringly, "You'll make it. You're a natural for diving because you don't lose your head. That's just about the only really dangerous thing a diver can do." He got into his harness, then picked up his movie camera in its underwater case.

At his signal, the four waded out into the cold water, splashed around a little to get accustomed to it, then put mouthpieces in place and prepared to don masks. Rick waited until last, and called, "Everybody getting air?" When they nodded, he put his own mouthpiece in place, checked to make sure the demand valve was working, then slipped the mask down from his forehead and went underwater.

There was a convenient sandy space among the rocks at the fifty-foot level. He reached it and turned to count noses. All were present. Visibility was good enough. He set his camera and took a position cross-legged on the sand. Barby and Scotty took similar positions and waited.

At Rick's signal, Jan slipped off her fins, which she placed carefully on the sand. Her weight belt followed, then her mask. Rick kept the camera going as she jerked the quick release buckle on her harness, then pulled the tank over her head, keeping the mouthpiece in place. At the last moment, she filled her lungs with air, let the mouthpiece drop to the sand, and swam away. Rick followed as she went about twenty feet into the rocks, and returned.

Jan had planned well. She picked up the mouthpiece and held it high so the air rushed out, then she popped it into her mouth and began breathing. She didn't bother with the tank harness yet. Instead, she picked up her mask, adjusted it, and blew it clear. Only then, when she could see and breathe, did she leisurely put the harness straps in position and swing the tank over her head and into place on her back. She buckled it on, and added her weight belt. The fins were last.

A flume of air from her exhaust, a sign of exhaustion, told Rick that Jan was tired. Probably the mental strain more than the exercise had left her too weak for further swimming. He slung the camera from a belt hook, took her hand and shook it solemnly, then led the way back to the beach.

After a short rest the others were anxious to go back in again, but Rick vetoed the idea. "We could," he admitted, "and probably no harm would come of it. But skin diving is the easiest thing in the world to overdo. Jan is tired. And she's excited, even if she doesn't look it. This afternoon, after we've had a little rest, we can come back again and just have fun. There won't be any strain on Jan then, because she passed the last test with flying colors. So she can swim without worrying whether she's meeting our standards, or doing it the way we think it ought to be done."

He grinned at the girl. "I know it was a strain. Remember, we've all been through it, too."

Jan had a nice smile. "You're right," she admitted. "I was so scared I wouldn't do it correctly! Then, when I knew that it was all right, I sort of fell apart."

Barby arose. "Come on, Jan. Let's go shower and change." She smiled with false sweetness at the boys. "Now that you're through testing Jan, I'm sure you won't mind doing your own work. 'Bye, now." And she left them to pick up the gear and truck it back to the laboratory building where it was kept.

Rick got to the shower first, then stretched out on his bed to wait for Scotty. It's a fine day, he told himself. All is well. JANIG has the island covered like a blanket. The project team is going full speed ahead. We're having fun. Jan is just the companion Barby needs. All's right with the world.

He turned over on his stomach and bunched his pillow up more comfortably. Then why, he asked himself, did he still feel funny?

Scotty came in from the shower, toweling vigorously. "What's eating you?" he demanded.

Rick turned over and stared at his pal. "Is it that obvious?"

"It is to me. What's up?"

"I don't know," Rick admitted. "Wish I did. Have you noticed how quiet everything is? It's like the day before a hurricane moves in. The ocean gets glassy, and there isn't any wind, and you're almost afraid to breathe because the air is so charged a breath might start the lightning."

" 'The calm before the storm,' " Scotty quoted. "Maybe it is. I feel it a little, too. But what can we do?"

Rick shrugged as expressively as one flat on his back could manage. "Nothing. We can swim with the girls, and we can keep working on the radio units. But there isn't a single thing to do so far as the project goes. I wish there were. I feel left out."

Scotty grinned. "You're never really happy unless we're up to our hips in trouble or a mystery. I know what's really bothering you. A fine, fat mystery is afoot and you haven't a shred of it you can call your own."

Rick had to grin back. There was much in what Scotty said. As long as the mystery of the two scientists remained unsolved, he wouldn't be really happy.

CHAPTER VII

The Peripatetic Barber

"We're trapped here," Barby said stormily, "and I want you to do something about it, Rick Brant! If you don't call Steve Ames and get permission for us to go to the mainland, I'll do it myself!"

Rick sighed. He had tried to point out that Barby was being illogical. Neither the Morrisons nor the Brants were trapped anywhere. It was just that common sense required the Morrisons to be careful.

Barby drove home another point. "Steve gave us a cover story, and what good is a cover story if you don't use it?"

Scotty grinned at Rick's expression of resignation. "Better give up," he advised.

Jan hadn't said anything. She just looked at Rick in a beseeching way that said as much as all Barby's arguments.

Rick shook his head unhappily. He knew when he was licked. Come right down to it, he didn't have the say-so on Jan leaving the island, anyway. He had taken a stand against her going to Whiteside, based half on intuition and half on the knowledge that a secret soon ceases to be one when it's flaunted in public. And Jan's presence was a part of the big secret of Spindrift.

He stood up and shrugged. "Chances are it will be all right. But if Jan is recognized by any of the enemy . . ."

"Steve isn't even sure there is an enemy," Barby pointed out swiftly. "How can you be so sure?"

Rick didn't answer. He turned and went into the house, the others at his heels. In the library, he consulted the schedule Steve had given them, so they would know where to reach him at any time. The agent was at JANIG headquarters in Washington today.

Rick got the number, and asked for Steve's extension. In a moment he had the agent on the wire.

"Let's scramble," he said, and threw the switch. Then, "Steve, Barby wants to take Jan to Whiteside. What do you think?"

Steve hesitated before he answered, "It's a little hard to give reasons why she shouldn't go, Rick. Have you checked her on the cover story?"

"Not yet. I will, though, if you say the word."

Again Steve hesitated, and Rick knew the agent was very much in his own position. There were no reasons to believe it would do any harm. Yet . . .

"Let her go," Steve said finally. "Only ask her and

THE PERIPATETIC BARBER 67

Barby not to get into any public parades. You know."

"I know," Rick affirmed. "All right, Steve. When is Marks coming?"

"We're not certain yet. Ask your father. Marks is having some trouble with the computations."

"Okay, Steve. See you soon." He hung up and turned to the others. "He says all right, but please don't get into any public parades. In other words, Barby, don't cover too much territory."

Scotty spoke up. "We'd better tell Duke and Jerry to leave it out of the paper."

Duke Barrows was editor and Jerry Webster the reporter for the Whiteside paper. Both were good friends. "They'll play ball," Rick agreed. "Well, young ladies, when is the big safari?"

Barby consulted her watch. "Right now. We'll dress and you can fly us over."

"Then right now means in an hour. Okay. We'll be ready."

Upstairs, Rick and Scotty washed up and changed into what Scotty called "shore-going clothes" that were only slightly less informal than their dungarees and T shirts. As they finished and sat down to wait for the girls, Rick picked up one of the radio units on the workbench. All were finished, although untested. A few final decorative touches remained for Barby's plastic headset, including setting in some rhinestones for her. It would look like any other plastic bauble when he finished.

"Let's get some fresh batteries while we're in

town," Rick suggested. "Then we can check these out tonight."

"Okay. And remind me to pick up a new mouthpiece for the lung Jan uses. She says the one that's on it now is too big and uncomfortable. It hurts her mouth."

Jan had become proficient under water with only a few hours practice. Rick had led the girls through the entire series of underwater maneuvers with the lungs, including practice in sharing one lung between them. He was satisfied that they both had a thorough understanding of team swimming and enough sense to stay out of at least the more obvious troubles novices can get into. He was content now to let them go off on their own, which they did fairly often.

After Rick's estimated hour the girls were ready —except that Barby had to make a phone call. She spent another fifteen minutes arranging a small get-together at a friend's home to introduce Jan to her chums.

"Now," she said brightly. "We're ready. Are you?"

Rick wisely refrained from comment.

Ten minutes later the four were in the Brants' car, en route to Barby's destination. Rick dropped the girls off and arranged to pick them up in two hours, then he turned the car toward town.

"Let's visit Duke and Jerry," he suggested.

Scotty looked at him. "Still bothered, aren't you?"

Rick shrugged. It was hard to pinpoint the way he

felt. He tried to put it into words. "I've talked to the scientists, including Parnell Winston. None of them has ever heard of an ailment like the thing that struck the team scientists. Winston especially knows a lot, because he's studied the human brain extensively. He doesn't even know of anything similar."

Scotty knew all this because he had been present. But talking aloud helped to make things clearer, so he only commented, "And where does that leave us?"

"At the starting line. We haven't moved an inch forward. But at least, if medical history seems to have no record of any such cases, we can assume that something new and different caused the scientists to go off the beam."

"Yes, but if some enemy caused it, how was it done?"

"Glad you asked that," Rick answered gloomily. "Wish someone could answer. Anyway, we know why it was done—if it was done. It was to cause trouble with the project. That would be important enough for an enemy to go to a lot of trouble."

Scotty shook his head. "The thing that sticks in my craw is, how come only two of the scientists got hit? Why wasn't the same thing used on the others? If anything was used, that is."

Rick was bothered by the same point, and he had no answer—nor did Steve Ames, with whom they had discussed the problem.

To both boys, the puzzle was more than just an

interesting problem to be solved. If some enemy really had penetrated the project and somehow caused disruption of the scientists' brains, then the people nearest and dearest to both of them were also in jeopardy. Spindrift now provided three out of five for the new project team.

Rick swung into the main street and into the public parking lot. The Whiteside *Morning Record* was in the heart of town, only a block away. Next to the parking lot was a hardware store where Rick planned to buy batteries, and diagonally across the street was the Sports Center. Nothing in Whiteside was far from anything else; it was a typical small town.

It took only a moment to buy a box of batteries; they were the type used in hearing aids. Then the boys crossed the street to the Sports Center. Extra mouthpieces for the lungs were in stock. They chose one that seemed softer and smaller than the regulation models, then started for the newspaper.

Two doors away from the Sports Center was the town's only barbershop. As they passed, Scotty suddenly grabbed Rick's arm and said hurriedly, "Come back!" Quickly he led the way out of sight of the barbershop windows.

Rick looked at him curiously. "See something?"

Scotty's forehead wrinkled. "I think so. But it's so unlikely that I'm not sure. Rick, I thought I saw the barber from Washington—the one with the massage machine!"

Rick focused the monocular on the barbershop

Rick's mouth opened in astonishment. "You're kidding!"

Scotty shook his head. "I'm not. I said I wasn't sure. But I don't want to stand in front and look, because if it is the barber, he'd recognize us."

Rick thought quickly. "Come on."

Back inside the Sports Center, he went to the manager and borrowed a powerful monocular—a pocket telescope that was really one half of a pair of binoculars. Then he and Scotty went across the street, taking care to keep out of sight of the barbershop by using parked cars as cover.

Rick found a vantage point behind a sedan that had all its windows open. He focused the monocular on the barbershop window.

Vince Lardner, the shop owner and—until now—the sole barber, was cutting the hair of a man Rick recognized as a local resident. A second barber was cutting the hair of another local man, but the barber had his back to the street for the moment.

Rick waited patiently. Scotty asked, "See anything?"

"Only his back. Wait a minute."

Presently the barber spun the chair around and walked to the sink. In a moment he turned and his face came into view in the tight close-up the powerful glass provided.

Rick sank his teeth into his lip and handed the glass to Scotty wordlessly.

The pieces were beginning to fall in place now, and the assumption that the project had been penetrated was a long step closer to proved fact.

The Washington barber had come to Whiteside!

"Wonder what he's after?" Scotty asked.

"One thing is for sure," Rick stated grimly. "He isn't here just to cut hair!"

CHAPTER VIII

The Mind Reader Strikes

JERRY WEBSTER often spoke of himself as "Whiteside's best reporter," which Rick considered a fair description, since he was the only reporter in town. Of course Duke Barrows, the editor, did some reporting himself, but that didn't count since he carried the title of managing editor.

"I'm a good reporter because I can sense a story," Jerry told Rick and Scotty. "You two have that certain look that spells trouble. What gives?"

"No trouble," Rick answered swiftly. "We just need a little help."

Duke Barrows glanced up from the proof sheets he was editing. "When Spindrift needs a little help, there's always a story in it. We'll make a deal, won't we, Jerry? You give us the story and we'll supply the help."

Rick knew Duke and Jerry well, so it wasn't necessary to beat around the bush. "No story. At least not yet, and I can't even give you a hint. Only we do need help."

"Two kinds," Scotty added.

"That's right. First of all, we have guests at Spindrift. Name of Morrison. You'll pick that up sooner or later, because Barby is running around town with Janice Morrison. What we need is a promise that you won't mention it in the paper."

Duke's eyebrows went up. "Ahah! Trying to suppress legitimate news, are you? What do you think, Jerry?"

Jerry Webster stared up at the ceiling. "I can see the headline now. 'Mysterious Visitors at Spindrift!' Lead paragraph: 'The mystery of strange visitors at Spindrift Island deepened today as members of the scientific foundation threatened the Whiteside *Morning Record* with drastic action unless the story was withheld.' How's that, Duke?"

"Needs editing," Duke replied, "but you're on the right track. What's the drastic action you're threatening us with?"

Scotty grinned. "Item," he intoned. "Editor and reporter drowned in own ink supply. Bodies found among leftover newspaper copies, apparently discarded with other waste."

"Too good for 'em," Rick disagreed. "How about 'Editor and reporter assume new dimensions. Rolled to paper thinness in own press.'"

"That's drastic," Duke admitted. "Seriously, Rick, you must have some good reason for asking us to leave out what could only be a small social item."

"It's a good reason, all right," Scotty answered him. "Only we can't tell you what it is, Duke."

The editor looked at Jerry. "What say, can we take it on faith?"

"Too simple," Jerry objected. "We ought to get something in trade."

Scotty made eating motions. "Apple pie, with homemade ice cream? Sunday night. Said apple pie would be used to pack down a nice, thick steak."

Jerry sighed. "I'm tempted."

"It's a deal," Duke agreed. "Make mine rare. And I add one thing: If there's a story, we get it first."

Rick looked pained. "Don't you always? But chances are, there never will be a story out of this."

"Government deal," Duke said. "It has to be. Okay, Rick. We'll go along. What's the second kind of help?"

Rick breathed a sigh of relief. He hadn't doubted that Duke and Jerry would hold the story, but it was always hard to ask a favor without being able to give the reason. "There's a new barber in Vince Lardner's shop."

"Think we're chumps who don't keep up with the news?" Jerry asked, his expression disdainful. "Of course there's a new barber. What of it?"

"We need some information about him. If you'll just let me see your notes, that should do it."

Jerry hesitated and Scotty grinned. "Bet he doesn't have any notes."

Duke glared at Jerry. "See? You've embarrassed the *Record*. I told you to get the story on that barber this morning."

"Time enough later," Jerry retorted, unruffled. "We don't need the dope until tonight, and I'll have it. What kind of information do you want?"

Rick listed the points on his fingers. "Where he came from, his full name, how he happened to get the job—I mean whether he applied directly to Vince or whether he got the job some other way—and how long he expects to stay."

Scotty had a few points, too. "If Vince had a vacancy, find out how long he looked for a barber, and how he got this one. Timing is important, Jerry. Get all you can on it. And ask him a few questions about his massage machine, if it's in sight. It looks like the hair gadgets they have in beauty shops."

Editor and reporter stared at the boys curiously. "Why so much interest in the barber?" Jerry demanded.

Rick tried to look casual. "Why, one of our special guests might want a haircut, and we couldn't take a chance that the barber might not be government approved. Simple."

Duke Barrows tilted back in his chair and pushed the green eyeshade to the top of his head. "I get the picture." He ticked off the points on his fingers, mocking Rick. "Strangers at Spindrift. Not to be mentioned. Government work of some kind, for sure, and pretty hot, too. So hot, in fact, that a stranger in

Whiteside might possibly be a menace to the strangers at Spindrift. Rick Brant asks help of local reporter. Gets name of stranger. Turns name and details in to some government security officer for a check. How's that?"

"Too good," Rick admitted. He had known it would be impossible to put anything over on Duke. The editor was a sharp cookie. "But keep it quiet, will you, please?"

"You know anything we discuss never goes farther than this office. All right, Rick. Jerry will get the dope. Hop to it, hawkeye. Duty calls."

Jerry waved his arms dramatically. "Hold the presses! New barber in town! Here I go, after the story of the year!" He swept through the door, then made a sheepish reappearance. "Forgot my pencil and copy paper," he explained, grabbed them, and vanished.

Duke waved the boys to chairs. "It will take a little while. Get comfortable. I have to finish this copy."

Rick and Scotty waited as patiently as possible. Scotty, the more relaxed of the pair, borrowed a copy of a style manual and studied it with apparent interest. Rick watched him, envious as always of his pal's ability to let time pass without floor pacing, nail chewing, or other impatient actions.

Duke's analysis of the situation was pretty good, Rick thought, and it was based on very little real information. He supposed that an editor had more experience to draw on than most people. But so did intelligence agents. It wasn't hard to see how a few information leaks could add up to a pretty clear picture in an agent's head.

Jerry was back in a short time. Apparently the interview hadn't taken long. He produced his sheaf of copy paper with a flourish and pounded on a desk for attention. The gesture wasn't necessary. Rick, Scotty, and Duke were waiting eagerly.

"Louis Collins, Journeyman Barber," Jerry read. "Age 43. Originally from St. Louis, most recently from Washington, D.C. Twenty-five years experience. Inventor of the Collins treatment for dry hair, which is the machine he has. Claims to have invented it five years ago, while working at a hotel in Washington. Came to Whiteside because he prefers being near the shore. He's an ardent fisherman. Saw Vince Lardner's ad in *The New York Times* a few days ago and applied at once by phone."

"What day and what time?" Rick asked quickly.

"Monday. He called about noon."

Scotty asked curiously, "How did you get that information out of him?"

"Nothing to it. I told Vince I'd like to look up his ad in the times, because he claimed the ad plugged Whiteside as an excellent climate. Then I told this new guy he must have moved fast to get in his application ahead of all the other applicants, and he said he hadn't even seen the *Times* until he went to lunch. He called right away. Vince nodded, so I guess the time worked out as Collins said it had. Vince said the ad had been running for a week, and no one else had applied."

Rick had been calculating. "Scotty, that means Collins phoned after we left Washington . . ." He stopped quickly.

Duke Barrows rubbed his hands in fiendish glee. "Ahah! Giving away information. So you've seen this Collins before, in Washington. No wonder you're worried about him. Jerry, I'll bet we can sell this information to some enemy for millions!"

Scotty grinned. "Not unless you have the plans for the death ray. Only death rays bring millions these days. Why, it's getting so a spy can't even sell atom bomb secrets for more than a buck apiece any more."

"Guess you're right," Duke admitted, crestfallen. "Well, Rick, anything else you need?"

"Middle initial or name?" Rick asked.

"M for Mayhew. Anything else?" Jerry asked with a superior air.

"That does it." Rick consulted his watch. "Let's go, Scotty. Time to pick up Barby. I won't thank you two, because you're going to get paid in steak and pie. See you later."

At the home of Barby's friend there was another wait while Rick chafed. He was anxious to get home and phone Steve Ames. However, as it developed, Steve couldn't be reached. It was after dinner before Rick made connections.

THE MIND READER STRIKES 81

He gave Steve the information Jerry had collected, then asked, "Isn't this proof of something?"

Steve chuckled. "It's proof that Whiteside has a new barber. That's all. But it's certainly strongly presumptive, Rick. We knew about Collins moving before you called, and we're continuing the check on him. Meanwhile, I'll alert my boys at Spindrift and tell them to keep on their toes."

"I'll pass the word," Rick offered.

"No need. I'm in touch by radio. Now, I want you to do something for me. Dr. Marks is arriving at Newark by train at six tomorrow morning. Tom Dodd is with him. Can you pick them up?"

"Sure. How?"

"Suppose you fly to Newark and have Scotty drive over. Then you can pick them up at the station by car and take them to the plane. If you fly them to Spindrift no one will know that Marks has even arrived. Tom will try to make sure no one is tailing him, and he'll help you to lose any cars that might try to follow."

"We can do it," Rick assured him. "I can land close to the city. I've done it before with pontoons."

"Good. Ordinarily, I'd have an agent meet them, but my Newark man is in the woods with the Boy Scout group. Call me when Marks is safely with the team."

"Will do," Rick promised.

Rick reported the conversation to his father when the scientist came in from late work in the laboratory. Hartson Brant nodded wearily. "Good. If Marks is on the way, that means he has answers we need badly to some of our mathematical problems."

"What I don't get is why he's coming on an overnight train," Scotty interjected. "That's doing it the hard way, because it's only a few hours from Washington to Newark. Why didn't he get a train at a decent hour? This way, he'll spend most of the night sitting on a siding somewhere."

The scientist smiled. "I gather that Marks has definite ideas of his own. I wouldn't care to be Tom Dodd. I'm sure Marks is giving him considerable trouble. He's convinced this security business is a plot to inconvenience him and the other people on the project."

"He didn't seem to have a very sweet disposition," Rick agreed. "Good night, Dad. Scotty and I are going to bed early, because we'll have to be up at dawn."

It was really the first sound night's sleep Rick had since the invasion of Spindrift by Steve and the Morrisons. Later, he had to smile at himself, because it seemed to be proof of what Scotty had said—that the real reason for his uneasiness was inactivity. He admitted that the problem of the stricken team members intrigued him. He made no claim to being any great shakes as a detective, but trying to solve mysteries, whether scientific or real, was a part of him.

Scotty departed first by boat a few minutes after

dawn. Rick warmed the Sky Wagon, then went in for a dish of cereal before taking off. He had plenty of time. Newark was only a few minutes away in the fast little plane.

He timed it perfectly. Scotty was just rolling up to the pier near Newark as Rick taxied in after landing. He got into a rowboat brought by an attendant, and tied the plane to an anchor buoy. In a moment he was in the car with Scotty.

"We'll get some excitement now," Rick predicted.

"Because Marks is arriving?"

"Yes, and because the barber has come to town. If he isn't up to his neck in this business, I'll eat his hair oil on pancakes."

Scotty shuddered. "You might at least wait until I've had more breakfast."

Rick ignored him. "Also, the team is now assembled in one place. That means the enemy has a single target to shoot at."

Scotty laughed out loud. "You should see yourself," he said, chuckling. "Since we found the barber yesterday, you've been a new man. Beaming and happy as can be. Now the enemy has a single target and you're pleased. Didn't it occur to you that the target is us, you simple meathead?"

"It did." Rick had to grin, too. "But who can locate the sharpshooter best? Why, the guy sitting on the bull's-eye."

Scotty parked and they walked into the station.

A quick check of the bulletin board told them the train was on time. They walked to the gate just as the train announcer called the arrival.

Tom Dodd was one of the last off. He had two suitcases under one arm, and he was supporting Marks with the other. Rick and Scotty ran to help. Was the scientist ill?

Scotty took the suitcases while Rick grabbed Marks' other arm. The scientist shook him off. "I'm perfectly all right," he said irritably. "Confound it! Rouse a man at the crack of dawn and expect him to respond like a ballet dancer to a cue. Nonsense!"

Marks' appearance belied his words. His face was drawn and pale, and it was obvious that his coordination wasn't very good. Tom Dodd was plainly worried.

"Let go of me," Marks demanded. He drew himself up and glared at the boys. "Which way is the car, please?"

"Straight ahead." Rick glanced at Dodd.

Marks stalked off, but his step was too careful to be convincing. He just wasn't normal.

"He wasn't like this when we got on the train," Dodd said in a low voice. "Let's get going. I'm anxious to get him to Spindrift."

In the parking lot, Rick ran to open the trunk so Scotty could stow the bags. Then he beckoned to Marks, who was staring straight ahead, his eyes glassy. "This is the car, sir."

Marks started for the open door. But instead of

bending down to get in, he walked straight ahead, rigid as a robot, and his face slammed into the edge of the low turret top.

Dodd caught him as he fell.

Rick jumped to the scientist's side, afraid he had been knocked out, and afraid, too, that something even more serious was wrong.

Marks was not unconscious, but his stare was fixed. "Are you all right, sir?" the boy asked anxiously.

The reply was unintelligible.

Scotty bent over the scientist, too. "Are you all right, sir?" he repeated urgently.

Marks' fixed stare never wavered. A spate of words poured from him, but they made no sense. Now and then a single word emerged clearly. Once it was "July," then "soup kettle" and "Planck's constant."

"Just like the others," Tom Dodd said helplessly.

Rick listened with horror. He had no doubt, no doubt at all. Steve had described it accurately, and here it was. Marks was a victim of the identical ailment that had stricken the other team members!

CHAPTER IX

Dagger of the Mind

Tom Dodd took command and gave orders crisply. "Help get him into the car. Here, into the back seat."

The agent got in after the scientist while the boys got into the front. "Scotty, start driving. We have to shake off any tail that picks us up. Try to find a stretch where there isn't much traffic."

Scotty swung the sedan into the traffic stream while Rick joined Tom Dodd in watching behind them. A few minutes later Scotty slipped into an alley and stepped on the gas. At the end of the alley he turned the wrong way down a one-way street, found another alley, and slipped into it. He emerged under a railroad trestle and moved into the stream of traffic once more. Watching carefully, he moved with the traffic until he saw an opportunity to cross a main thoroughfare as the light changed from yellow to red.

Theirs was the last car through the intersection,

Rick saw, before traffic started through the cross street. Scotty took another turn, doubled back, and went through another alley. As he emerged onto a street where traffic was sparse, he slowed.

"That should do it," Tom Dodd said. "Nice work."

"How is he?" Rick asked anxiously.

"Just like the others," Tom said flatly. "Listen, boys. Our Newark agent is in Whiteside. I don't think it's wise to take Marks to Spindrift in this condition, but I don't want to take him far, either. Have you any contacts here?"

Rick tried to remember. His father had associates in Newark, he was sure, including a doctor or two. But he couldn't remember their names. "I could call home," he suggested. "Dad will have some ideas."

Dodd considered. "You couldn't use the scrambler from here. Could you tip your father off without giving information to anyone who happened to be listening on the wire?"

Rick thought he could.

"Okay." Dodd motioned to a restaurant. "There's a phone in there. I can see the booth through the window. Hop to it."

Rick hurried into the restaurant. The full horror of what had happened to Dr. Marks was just having its effect. He found himself shivering as though with a severe chill. Marks was the victim of something ghastly. He seemed to be trying to make sense, as though there was still a glimmer of intelligence behind the blank stare. But his words were disconnected, completely unintelligible.

Barby answered the phone, caught the urgency in Rick's voice, and yelled for their father. Hartson Brant came hurriedly.

"What is it, Rick?"

"Guarded language," Rick said urgently. "Dad, don't you have a professional friend in Newark? The teletype machine just went haywire for the third time and I need help."

Hartson Brant muttered, "Good Lord! Yes, Rick. I have a mechanic friend who is ideally suited for the purpose. Constantine Chavez. Look him up in the professional part of the phone directory. I'll phone him and say you're bringing the machine."

"Good, Dad. I'll come home as soon as possible. Better phone the man who runs the machines and give him the information."

"All right. Be careful."

Rick disconnected and looked up the name under the listing of physicians. Back in the car, he cast a quick look at Dr. Marks. The scientist was sitting quietly, staring straight ahead. He wasn't talking, and Rick was glad. He didn't know how much of the gibberish he could take. It was weird and horrifying, particularly since Marks had been so crisp and terse—even though sometimes unpleasant—in his speech.

Dr. Chavez was watching for them through his window and hurried out to meet the car. He was a tall, slender man with handsome features that showed his Spanish ancestry.

"You must be Rick," he said, shaking hands. "You look very much like your father. He phoned to say you were bringing a damaged machine, but I also gathered he was merely being cautious about something he didn't care to discuss on the phone."

"That's right, Doctor," Rick said. He introduced Tom Dodd and Scotty, failing to mention that Dodd was a government agent. Then he pointed to Dr. Marks in the back seat.

"There's your patient, sir."

"Bring him into the house," Dr. Chavez directed. "I assume from his appearance that the trouble is mental and not physical?"

"Exactly," Dodd said.

Inside the house they found one room outfitted as a home office. "I have an office downtown," the doctor explained, "but I also use this one a few afternoons a week. Now, who can tell me about this?" His eyes were on Marks, and as he talked, he reached for the scientist's wrist.

Tom Dodd explained carefully, "He was suddenly stricken. We were with him. We don't know what happened, except that he made sense one minute, but talked only garbled words the next."

Chavez took an otoscope, an instrument used to examine eyes, ears, nose, and throat, and switched on the tiny light. He flicked it into Marks' eyes and watched the behavior of the pupils. Then he listened with a stethoscope. A little rubber hammer came out next and was applied to the reflexes of the stricken scientist. The reflexes looked normal to Rick.

Dr. Marks suddenly looked up and began spouting gibberish. Rick winced.

Chavez listened gravely, apparently not at all disturbed. The flow of meaningless words ceased and Rick sighed with relief. He saw that Scotty had been equally affected.

"What is your specialty, Doctor?" Dodd asked.

"I'm a neurologist."

That was good, Rick thought. A neurologist was exactly what Marks seemed to need.

"Do you make anything of this?" Dodd asked.

The doctor shook his head. "Nothing. I've never seen a case like it. I've never even heard of one. In fact, I know of only one analogue, and it's an electronic one. Do you know how computers work? The big electronic brains?"

The three nodded.

"Then you will understand. I have worked with computers, and now and then one of them suddenly starts turning out gibberish for no apparent reason. A check of the circuits may show that everything is functionally normal. Yet, the gibberish continues. Often it clears up, with no more reason than it started. Sometimes this happens when the machine is cold, before it is properly warmed up. At other times, it happens when the machine is tired."

"Tired?" Dodd looked his disbelief. "Machines don't get tired. Not in those terms."

Chavez smiled. "Perhaps not. Yet, to those who work with them, it does sometimes appear that the machine is tired. There is really no other expression for it."

Rick knew something of this through his association with Dr. Parnell Winston of the Spindrift staff. Winston was an expert in the new science of cybernetics, which is defined as the science of communications and control mechanisms in both living beings and machines.

"Parnell Winston would know," Rick said.

"He most certainly would," Chavez agreed. "Are you aware that he and I have worked together? My interest was in the biological portion of the project. His was in the electronic. Of course we worked as a team with other specialists."

"Under whose auspices?" Dodd asked quickly.

"Let us be candid," Chavez invited. "Obviously, this is not an ordinary case. The guarded language Hartson Brant used was indication enough of that. Rick Brant I identify because of his resemblance to my friend, and I think I identify Don Scott, of whom I have heard a great deal from Hartson. But who are you, Mr. Dodd?"

For answer, Tom Dodd took out his identification folder and handed it to the physician.

Chavez studied it. "I know your organization, Mr. Dodd. But what is of greater importance for the moment, your organization knows me. I suspect it was for that reason Hartson Brant selected me for you to consult." He gestured to the phone. "You will want to call your office. My records are in New York."

Dodd's face expressed his relief. "I was a little nervous," he admitted. "It was a choice between possibly risking further damage to Marks or taking a chance on someone based only on a recommendation from Dr. Brant. I'm glad you're in the clear."

He went to the phone and called New York. In a moment he said, "Dodd here. Check on Dr. Constantine Chavez." He held the phone for perhaps half a minute, then said, "Roger. That does it."

He held out his hand to the neurologist. "Glad to know you, Doctor. Can you take over?"

"Not only can I take over, you would have trouble getting rid of me. This man is obviously hurt in a way that is strange to me, and I assure you, my experience with damaged minds is considerable. He may be somewhat under the influence of a drug—I will check more thoroughly—but that is not the cause. If I may make a quick and highly tentative guess, this mind is suffering from some kind of trauma induced from an outside source."

"You mean it's not a disease?" Rick asked quickly.

"Precisely. I know of no disease that would behave like this. I can't even imagine a disease with these symptoms."

"How can you be sure?" Scotty pressed.

"Obviously I can't at this stage of investigation. But you must recognize that a physician develops a rather definite feeling for injury after years of experience. My own experience tells me that mental damage of this scope is almost always accompanied by other symptoms when it is the product of a disease. No, I cannot credit the idea of a pathogenic organism too seriously. It is as though some outside agent pierced the cranium and cut off the control centers of the brain."

"A dagger of the mind," Scotty murmured.

Chavez looked up sharply. "Yes! An ideal phrase for it."

Rick recognized the quotation from his schoolwork. *Macbeth,* Act II. Another of Shakespeare's phrases from the same work leaped into his mind. "Macbeth hath murdered sleep." Not Macbeth, but Marks. Rick knew he wouldn't sleep well that night, nor for many nights to come.

Dagger of the mind! Well, it fitted. Watching the blank face of what had been, only hours before, a brilliant scientist, Rick could feel its deadly point himself.

CHAPTER X

Search for Strangers

THE good weather turned bad, and dark clouds hung low over the New Jersey coast. It was appropriate weather for the state of mind at Spindrift. With Marks a victim of the mysterious "dagger of the mind," only Dr. Morrison remained of the original team.

The question, of course, was "Who next?"

At Hartson Brant's urgent request, Steve Ames visited the island and a meeting of all staff was called in the big library.

Rick and Scotty sat on a library table, while the scientists occupied the few library chairs. Steve Ames sat on Hartson Brant's desk and acted as chairman for the informal session.

By mutual agreement, the girls had been excluded. Jan was nearly in a state of shock over what had happened to Marks. Not only was she fond of the crusty scientist, but she was fearful that the mysterious ailment would strike her father next. And Barby was rapidly catching the same fear. After all, new team members probably were not immune, and Hartson Brant, Julius Weiss, and Parnell Winston were deeply involved in the project.

Steve called the meeting to order. "Hartson, you suggested that I come, which I was glad to do. Suppose you start by telling us what you had in mind."

"Very well, Steve." The scientist's glance embraced his colleagues and the boys.

"We have a problem that must be solved before we can continue with calm and objective minds on the project that faces us. The problem is simply, what is the ailment that has stricken three of us, and what is its cause?"

Hartson Brant tamped tobacco into his pipe thoughtfully. "Let us see what we know. First of all, two team members were stricken in Washington, within a short time of each other. They were examined by competent specialists who arrived at no conclusion. They admitted they were unable to diagnose the ailment. The possibility of an unknown disease was considered briefly, but not seriously. The possibility of a chemical agent—a drug, if you like—also was considered. This possibility has not been entirely rejected. However, a detailed laboratory investigation disclosed no trace of chemicals in the patients, apart from chemicals that were expected, of course."

"Could there be chemicals that left no trace?" Scotty asked.

Hartson Brant shook his head. "No one can claim total knowledge of body chemistry, obviously. Just the same, the elements to be found in the body, and the proportions in which they occur, are well known. I said the possibility has not been entirely eliminated, but it seems unlikely that chemical interference caused the disruption."

"What does that leave?" Steve inquired.

The scientist shrugged. "I can't even guess. Physical interference, perhaps. There is also a possibility, which is very difficult to explore, that the ailment was caused within the minds of the scientists by some catalytic agent, or by some psychic trauma that we can't even imagine."

Rick and Scotty exchanged glances. They had seen the ailment at work, and even its effects were almost beyond description. Its cause was hard to imagine.

"But, to continue. Steve recognized the possibility that the ailment was caused by some outside source. Call it an enemy source, if you prefer. He acted to get the remaining team members beyond reach of the enemy by smuggling them to Spindrift. He succeeded with Dr. Miller—excuse me, Dr. Morrison. He did not succeed with Dr. Marks. What does this suggest?"

"That hiding Dr. Morrison was an effective preventative," Steve Ames concluded.

"If he is hidden." Rick said the words before he even thought.

"What do you mean, Rick? No one outside the family or the project knows of his presence!" Julius Weiss exclaimed.

Steve held up his hand. "Hold it a minute. We'll get to that point in its proper turn."

Hartson Brant picked up the threads again. "We will assume for the moment that Steve's statement is correct, and that hiding Dr. Morrison was a preventative. I know Steve doesn't accept this fully, but we must use assumptions since we have no facts of consequence. If the assumption is correct, then we have to accept the fact that enemy agents are interested in the project. And we must also accept that they have some means of creating a mental block by remote control."

Rick stole a glance at Parnell Winston. The cyberneticist was sitting quietly, his bushy eyebrows knitted thoughtfully. Winston hadn't said a word.

Hartson Brant paced the floor as he went on. "We now have one slight bit of additional information that supports the theory of enemy interference. You are all aware of what happened to Dr. Marks this morning. He is in the hands of Constantine Chavez, who is in touch with the physicians in charge of the other team members. Dr. Chavez is of the opinion that Dr. Marks' mental injury was caused by physical means, although he cannot say how. He also states, although there seems to be no connection with the mental injury, that Marks was drugged."

Parnell Winston spoke for the first time. "Steve, if Chavez says Marks was drugged, we can accept it. How could it have happened?"

Steve spread his hands in a gesture that seemed to Rick to indicate embarrassment. "I have gone over every step of the journey with Tom Dodd. The answer is yes. Thanks to Marks' bullheadedness, and a clerical error, there was an opportunity for an enemy to get at him on the train."

The scientists waited, obviously wanting to know more. Steve elaborated. "Marks was covered by one of our men at every moment, even while he was working at the Bureau of Standards, and while he was at his apartment. The agents ate and drank the same things. Nothing has happened to them. However, when the reservations were made for the train trip, Marks specified that he wanted a bedroom. He got one, and Tom Dodd got the one next door."

"Why did Marks want to travel by train overnight, anyway?" Scotty demanded. "That's getting from Washington to Newark the hard way."

"I told you he was stubborn," Steve reminded. "Tom tried to talk him out of it but failed. After all, the project team members aren't prisoners. We can't use force, and we can't order them to do anything. Marks wanted to go overnight by train because he always traveled that way, he said. He insisted."

Dr. Morrison said sadly, "I assure you that he is

not an easy man to get along with sometimes. But we must remember that he is—or was—an extremely competent scientist. Competence like his can be forgiven many eccentricities."

"Thanks to his eccentricities, we've also lost his competence," Julius Weiss pointed out. "Go on, Steve."

"Right. Well, Tom specified bedrooms A and B, and by the time he got the reservations and found that he had actually received bedrooms B and C, it was too late to change because the train was sold out."

"I can't see what difference that made," Rick objected.

"You will. People often buy connecting bedrooms on a train, and that's what Tom had done. He planned to keep the connecting door open and remain awake all night with an eye on Marks. However, while A and B connect, B and C do not. Do I make myself clear?"

"I think so," Rick agreed. "The connecting bedrooms come in pairs, A-B, C-D, and so on."

"That's it. Well, Tom ran a fast check on the person who had received bedroom D, and found it was a Baltimore businessman who often traveled on the same train, going overnight to New York. So Tom didn't worry about it. Instead, he kept his bedroom door open so he could watch the corridor. He says he didn't sleep at all, and I believe him. He's one of my best agents. The occupant of Bedroom D came on the train at Baltimore and went right to bed. The night passed quietly, until it was time to get Marks up. Tom had great trouble waking him up, and he was groggy until this strange effect hit him. Rick and Scotty know. They were there."

The boys shuddered, remembering Marks' condition.

"But where did the opportunity to drug him come in?" Weiss asked.

"We've done some fast checking on every possible angle," Steve said quietly, "and we've found a couple of interesting things. First of all, the man who reserved Bedroom D is in a Baltimore hospital. He was struck by a hit-and-run car as he walked from his office to the railroad station. Obviously, he was struck deliberately. He's in critical condition."

"Then the man on the train . . ." Rick gasped.

"Yes. Who was the man on the train? We don't know. We've had our Boston office go over the room, and they've turned up no fingerprints except those of the porter who cleaned up after the train left New York. The room was wiped clean. But our Boston men also found an interesting spot on the rug. They had a sample analyzed, and so far as we can determine, it's a kind of water-soluble salt paste often used by doctors when they take electrocardiograms."

The group leaned forward, interested. Rick knew the kind of stuff Steve meant, because he had once watched Zircon getting an electrocardiogram. The big scientist had fainted from sheer overwork, and possible heart complications were suspected. The technician squeezed the paste from a tube and applied it to wrists, ankles, and chest, under the metal terminals of the machine. Its purpose was to allow a better electrical contact.

Julius Weiss demanded excitedly, "Steve, do you imply that this unknown person took an electrocardiogram of Marks' heart responses?"

The JANIG agent shrugged. "I imply nothing. I'm merely reporting."

Again Parnell Winston spoke. "Perhaps I can shed some light on this. It's true that such an electropaste is used to make better connections for electrocardiograms. But perhaps of greater importance for this discussion, it is also used in making electroencephalograms."

Rick and Scotty spoke in unison. "What?"

Winston turned to them. "It's a long word, but not a difficult one. *Electro* for electrical. *Encephalo* is simply a Greek form meaning 'the brain.' *Gram*, also from the Greek, means something drawn or written. A record, if you like. So an electroencephalogram is simply an electrical recording of the brain."

"That may be significant," Hartson Brant said thoughtfully. "But, assuming an enemy could get an EEG—which is the handy way of saying electroencephalogram, Rick and Scotty—what would he do with it?"

Parnell Winston rose. "Hartson, I think you can conduct the rest of this without me. I have an extraordinary notion whirling around in my head that I'd like to discuss with Chavez. I'll pick up the car at the pier and drive over, if you don't mind." And by the way, Steve, can JANIG get some information for me?"

"We can try."

"Good. I want to know if the two team scientists who were stricken first had EEG's made after the attack. I would also like to check their medical history, as completely as possible, to find out if EEG's were ever taken while they were normal."

"I'll give the orders right away," Steve agreed. "I don't know what we can turn up on their early medical history, but we can try."

Parnell Winston departed. Rick almost wished he had asked permission to accompany Winston, but there was more to be said here, too.

"The evidence is not conclusive," Hartson Brant summed up, "but it is certainly strong enough to warrant a clear assumption: we have an enemy who, by unknown means, can inflict brain damage."

"All right. Now for some loose ends." Steve looked at the boys. "Rick and Scotty turned up a barber in Whiteside. It happened they had first seen him in the project office building in Washington, so they got his name and called. We were already checking on the barber, and knew he was in Whiteside. We'll dig deeper until we know more about him than he does. But for now, our information indicates he is just what he claims to be. He got the job in Whiteside legitimately. He had planned to take a new job for a long time. So far as we can tell, he's as innocent as a woolly little lamb."

"Just the same," Rick said stoutly, "I'm not satisfied. I'd like to get some more dope on that massage machine of his. Especially after what Dr. Winston said."

Steve grinned. "Why don't you?"

Rick and Scotty looked at each other, and rose to the challenge. "We will," they stated flatly.

Steve nodded. "All right. You're known in Whiteside and my men are not. An influx of strangers, or even one inquisitive stranger, would attract attention. But that's not all. I have another job for you, too."

They waited eagerly.

"I want a survey of the area. My Boy Scout team can help somewhat, but they're strangers, too, even though they have an explanation for their presence. Scan the area for anything suspicious. Get your newspaper pals on the job and have them sniff around for evidence of any strange folks in the area. They can do it easily."

"We'll do it," Rick agreed. There was nothing hard about looking for strangers in their own territory. He knew exactly how to go about it.

"All right. Search for strangers. Get your pals on the job, but do it without tipping anything off.

That State Police captain you've worked with will be a big help, too. You can tell him national security is involved, but that's all."

"At least we're not working entirely in the dark any more," Dr. Morrison said wearily. "Even if the assumption of an enemy is wrong, it's something to go on."

Rick stood up. The conference apparently was at an end.

"Tonight we'll plan," he announced. "And tomorrow we'll start. If there are any strangers in the area, you'll have full particulars by tomorrow night."

"That," said Steve Ames, "is a promise I'll hold you to."

CHAPTER XI

The Dangerous Resemblance

Rick stirred, and whatever he had been dreaming faded into vagueness. He couldn't have said what he had been dreaming about. He was neither asleep nor awake, but in the shadowland somewhere between. Something as yet undefined had brought him halfway toward awakening, but the influence was not powerful enough to bring his senses alert.

And then, suddenly, he was wide awake, ears straining to listen. He sensed a presence in the room, and even as he tried to recognize it, a form landed on his chest and steel spikes drove into his ribs. He leaped up with a yell as another form landed on the bed. Both forms were making fantastic noises.

His eyes opened wide as he suddenly realized that a rousing cat-dog fight was taking place on his stomach!

Scotty ran in and leaped for the battlers. He grabbed the spitting, snarling cat and held it high.

Dismal let out a wail of anguish as he realized his hated enemy was out of reach.

Rick shouted, "Down, boy!"

Dismal leaped high and landed again with four feet bunched on Rick's stomach.

Rick's shout died into a gurgle. Not that the pup was heavy, but he had landed while his master was in the midst of a breath, with muscles relaxed.

Scotty put the cat into the hall and closed the door, trapping Dismal in the room. Then he turned and laughed at Rick's discomfort.

"Next time you arrange a fight for your personal entertainment, you'd better have a referee on hand."

"It was a draw," Rick said ruefully, "except that the innocent bystander lost. Whatever got into Dismal?"

Scotty was dressed. Apparently he had already been downstairs. "The cat went too far. Dismal found him drinking from his water dish."

Rick grinned. That was adding insult to injury, all right. He stripped off the blankets and examined his stomach. Shah's claws had dug right through blanket, sheet, and pajamas, but had not drawn blood.

"It was time to get up, anyway," he said philosophically. "Gangway, Scotty. I'm going to shower and dress. We've got work to do."

"Uhuh. The passengers are waiting downstairs," Scotty said.

Rick blinked. "What passengers?"

"Jan and Barby. They want to go."

THE DANGEROUS RESEMBLANCE 107

The boys had decided the evening before that they would start the search with a flight in the Sky Wagon. After a quick inspection of the area, which probably wouldn't disclose much, they planned to go into Whiteside for a talk with Jerry and Duke at the newspaper office, and with Captain Douglas of the State Police.

Rick considered. He didn't mind taking the girls around on pleasure junkets, but this was business. "Why do they have to go?" he demanded.

Scotty shrugged. "They don't. But Jan is plenty upset over Dr. Marks, and Barby is starting to worry about Dad and the others. If we leave them here, they'll just stew. If they go, it may take their minds off things."

"I suppose that's right. Anyway, they can't get in the way much. We'll stick 'em in the back seat."

"Come on, then. Let's eat and get going."

Rick showered and dressed hurriedly, and got downstairs just in time to take his seat at the breakfast table. After bidding the family good morning, he turned to Jan. "Shah and Dismal had a fight this morning."

Jan put a hand to her mouth. "Oh! Shah didn't hurt him, did he?"

That nettled Rick a little. The idea of assuming that a mere cat, even a champion Persian, could win a fight with Dismal! Then common sense got the better of him. The unhappy truth was, Shah could lick Dismal with no strain at all.

"No damage," he replied. "Except to me. The war took place on my stomach."

Jan was supposed to look sorry, but she didn't. She giggled. Barby giggled, too.

"I guess they thought you'd be a fair witness if anyone asked who won," Jan explained.

Rick saw he was getting no sympathy. After all, what could anyone do? Dogs and cats were just natural enemies. Besides, if he was fair about it, he had to admit that Shah teased the pup but didn't start serious fights.

After breakfast the four young people went down to the beach where the Sky Wagon was hauled up. In a few moments they were air-borne. Rick headed for Seaford, the fishing town down the coast. It didn't make much sense to go farther south than that. Beside him, Scotty polished the binocular lenses with a piece of lens tissue from the camera kit, and started sweeping the area below.

Apparently all was normal along the seacoast and in Seaford, but that meant nothing. The area could be loaded with strangers and they'd never know it from the air.

Rick had a sudden idea. "Let's call Cap'n Mike and get him on the job. If there are any strangers in Seaford, he'll know it."

"I think that's a wonderful idea," Barby called from the back seat.

Jan asked, "Who is Cap'n Mike?"

Barby immediately related the adventure of

Smugglers' Reef, and the part the retired fishing skipper had played.

Cap'n Mike knew everything worth while about the town of Seaford. He would be a good check point not only for the town, but also for the summer colonies between Whiteside and Seaford. He often acted as a fishing guide for the summer tourists.

Rick checked the summer colonies from the air, although he had little expectation of seeing anything unusual.

Barby pointed down as they passed over one. "Look! Scotty, let me have the glasses."

Both boys turned quickly. "What do you see?" Scotty asked. He handed her the glasses.

"The gaudiest houseboat!" Barby exclaimed. "Jan, it's painted orange!"

The boys snorted.

After inspecting the coast from Seaford past Spindrift to the more populated areas on the north, Rick swung inland to inspect the woods near Whiteside. He didn't know exactly what to look for, except possibly unexplained campfires that could be investigated later.

He landed at Spindrift and went at once to the house. Cap'n Mike didn't have a phone, but Rick knew how to get a message to him. Scotty, listening, said, "He won't be in. The fleet is still out fishing this time of day."

Rick grinned. "It's Sunday. Lost track of time?"

Scotty had. But suddenly he snapped his fingers. "Hey! Duke and Jerry are coming over for dinner."

His message to Cap'n Mike en route through a mutual friend, Rick motioned to Scotty. "Let's go."

They took both of the island boats, planning to leave one for Duke and Jerry to use later in the day. Then, after tying up the boats at the main pier and getting the car, they called first on Captain Douglas of the State Police.

The officer knew the boys well, and knew in addition of their connection with JANIG. He promised readily to assist.

"Probably my own officers won't be too much help," he said, "but they can ask the local police to keep their eyes open up and down the coast. We won't say anything about the federal government being interested. To everyone but me, this will be a routine State Police matter."

Rick hesitated for a moment, but he was sure of Captain Douglas' discretion. "We're interested in the new barber, too," he added. "Steve Ames is already checking him, but you might keep your eyes open."

"I'll do that," Captain Douglas assured him. "And how about the Boy Scout leaders camped behind Spindrift?"

Rick was about to say casually that he didn't suspect any Boy Scout leaders, then he caught the twinkle in the captain's eye.

"He's hep," Scotty said.

THE DANGEROUS RESEMBLANCE 111

Captain Douglas nodded. "One of my officers paid them a call. He's a sharp one, and he made some kind of excuse for getting into their tent. He came back and reported they were apparently on a hunting expedition of some kind—with riot guns. I took a car full of armed troopers and we dropped in. One of the Scout leaders turned out to be a man who was in the same FBI class that I attended. He showed me his identification card, so I gave him my phone number in case he needed help. And that was that."

Scotty said thoughtfully, "I guess the hardest thing in the world is keeping a secret."

"That's the second hardest," Douglas corrected. "The hardest usually is finding out how the secret became public in the first place."

The boys went from the State Police barracks to the Whiteside *Morning Record* and found Jerry on the job. "The press never sleeps," he greeted them. "What brings you two to town on a peaceful Sunday?"

"We brought you a boat," Rick explained. "In exchange for a favor."

Jerry eyed them suspiciously. "What kind of a favor?"

It took only a moment to explain. "Sure," Jerry agreed. "Duke won't object to keeping you posted. We'll keep an eye open for you. And we'll collect for the favor with an extra helping of pie tonight."

"It's a deal," Rick agreed.

As it turned out, Jerry's bargain of an extra helping of pie was conservative. He had three for dessert that night.

Rick noticed that both Jerry and Duke eyed Dr. Morrison curiously, and he knew they were trying to recall if they had ever seen a picture that would help place him in their minds. Not that they would use the information. It was just that newspapermen developed a high order of frustration in the face of a mystery.

But Jan noticed something else. She came over to where Rick was pouring fresh coffee for his friends. "Rick, those friends of yours are nice. Have you noticed how much Mr. Barrows looks like Dad?"

Rick looked. The two were deep in conversation, and it was the first time he had seen them together. They looked very much alike, particularly in the gathering darkness. They were about the same height, give or take a fraction of an inch, and both had the same shock of unruly hair. They probably weighed within five pounds of each other. Actually, however, the resemblance was superficial. They might have been cousins, but not brothers.

"They do look alike," Rick agreed.

Later, he saw Jan deep in conversation with Jerry and wandered by, to eavesdrop a little. He knew that Jerry was entirely trustworthy, but his friend was also a nosy reporter who would try to pump the girl. Rick intended to step in and break it up if that were the case.

THE DANGEROUS RESEMBLANCE 113

"The Virgin Islands sound wonderful," Jerry was saying. "How long did Rick and the others stay with your family?"

"They never actually stayed with us," Jan replied. "Of course we invited them to, but they were so anxious to get to Clipper Cay, they only stayed one night in town. We met them that night, at Dr. Ernst's. He's a mutual friend. I was excited about the treasure, and I begged Dad to take Mother and me to Clipper Cay, so I could dive with the boys. He was going to take us, too, only everyone was back in Charlotte Amalie with the treasure before we had a chance."

Rick grinned and went on his way. Jan was talking with great assurance. He didn't have to worry about Jerry breaking down the cover story.

It was late when the party broke up. Rick and Scotty took their guests to Whiteside Pier, where Duke had left his car. As they roared up to the pier Rick had to swerve to avoid a pram, a blunt-ended rowboat, that had been tied carelessly in the place where he usually tied up. He wondered who owned it. Prams were not usual along the coast.

Jerry and Duke climbed out after thanking the boys again for a fine dinner. The two walked off into the darkness toward the parking lot.

Rick started to back out and head for home, then paused. He was curious about the pram.

"Hand me the boat hook," he told Scotty.

His pal obliged. "What's up?"

"I'm curious. Who around here has a pram?"

"No one I know. That looks like a new one, too."

Rick pulled the little rowboat closer with the boat hook and turned the speedboat's searchlight on it, hoping to find a name.

Suddenly both boys froze.

"Was that a yell?" Rick asked.

Scotty was already on his way up the pier. "Yes, from the parking lot. Come on!"

Rick hurriedly threw a rope around a piling and secured it with a couple of fast half-hitches, then he hurried after Scotty.

It was pitch dark in the parking lot, but they could hear sounds of a scuffle plainly now, and once there was a muffled grunt.

It suddenly occurred to Rick that he hadn't heard Duke's car start. He sprinted, calling to Scotty to look for a weapon. Once, some time ago, they had fought a battle with rocks against guns in this very spot. He scooped up a couple of rocks, hoping no guns were waiting this time.

"Hold 'em!" Scotty yelled. "We're coming!"

There was a yell in reply. Jerry Webster called, "Watch it! They're running away!"

Car headlights switched on, and in their glare Rick saw Jerry pointing. For a moment he considered following his friends' assailants, then abandoned the idea. They could escape easily in the woods.

"What happened?" Scotty demanded.

"I'm curious. Who around here has a pram?"

116 THE ELECTRONIC MIND READER

Duke Barrows got out of the car, nursing his head.

"Two men jumped us when we started to get into the car," he answered shakily. "One smacked me on the head with something hard and almost knocked me out. If Jerry hadn't put up a good fight, they'd have had us—although I don't know what for."

"Were they holdup men?" Rick asked quickly.

"They didn't wear signs," Duke answered grumpily. "But holdup men usually say something, don't they? 'This is a stickup.' Or something like that."

Jerry Webster examined bruised knuckles in the glare of the car head lamps. "They didn't say anything," he added. "Not a word. When you yelled, they broke off and ran into the woods."

Scotty scratched his head. "Mighty funny," he mused. "What could they have wanted?"

Duke Barrows brushed dirt off his jacket. "They probably were reporters from a Newark paper," he said caustically, "trying to find out about the mysterious visitors on Spindrift."

It hit Rick then. "Duke," he exclaimed, "you look like Dr. Morrison! I'll bet it was a case of mistaken identity!"

The editor looked at him keenly. "Could be," he agreed. "That means you have reason to believe someone would be interested in harming Dr. Morrison."

"I'm just assuming," Rick said hurriedly.

"Uh-hum." The editor grunted his disbelief. "And what should we do about it?"

Rick looked at Scotty, who shrugged. The shrug said that probably nothing could be done now, so far as Duke and Jerry were concerned, but that the case was far from closed.

"Better notify Captain Douglas," Rick suggested. "I can't think of anything else."

Jerry Webster flexed an arm that appeared to be aching. "Sure that won't conflict with your security people?" he asked.

Rick assumed an air of wide-eyed innocence. "Now, Jerry! Who said anything about security people? I just suggested you notify the State Police. Who else would you notify when someone attacks you?"

Duke climbed into the car. "Come on, Jerry. We'll get no satisfaction out of these two. Let's go rub liniment on our wounds, and then we'll make a report to the State Police. Good night, lads. And I hope your mystery bites you. Let me know if it does, so I can say 'I told you so' in print."

The boys waved as Duke drove off, leaving them in darkness. As they made their way back to the speedboat, Rick spoke his thoughts aloud.

"I guess the enemy uses muscles, too, huh?"

Scotty answered thoughtfully, "Looks like it. Unless they really were holdup men."

Rick shook his head, even though Scotty couldn't

see the reaction. "Pretty unlikely. But suppose the enemy kept a watch on movements in and out of Spindrift? From a distance they might assume that Duke was Morrison. So it would make sense for them to keep a watch at the pier in case he came back—which he did."

"And when he came back, they'd either murder him or kidnap him?" Scotty sounded disbelieving. "I doubt it. Nothing the enemy has done so far points to that kind of tactic. Why should they start using muscle methods now?"

Rick had no good answer. "Let's step on it," he said. "We have to report this. I have a hunch the Boy Scout team is going to be scouring the woods around here tonight."

CHAPTER XII

The Coast Guard Draws a Blank

Rick said quietly, "And so the wolf ate Little Red Riding Hood, and when the grandmother heard about it she said—"

Barby's voice erupted in the tiny earphone plug in Rick's ear. "I don't think that's very funny, Rick Brant!"

Scotty spoke up. "Barby doesn't like realism in her fairy tales."

Barby answered, "I don't think you're very funny either, Donald Scott!" Her voice faded on the last word.

Rick asked quickly, "Barby, did you move then?"

"No, Rick. Why?"

"You faded. Scotty, did you notice a fade?"

"Negative. I did not."

Rick asked, "Barby, please recite something."

"Recite what?"

"Anything."

Barby began, "She walks in beauty like the night . . ."

Rick turned slowly, listening for differences in strength of signal received.

Scotty interrupted. "Hey, what's that?"

"Lord Byron," Barby said loftily. "I wouldn't expect you to know."

Rick had it now. "Okay," he called. "Come on in."

He had been standing on the front porch of the Brant home. Scotty was inside the laboratory building, while Barby and Jan were at Pirate's Field. Presently Scotty joined him and grinned. "Work good?"

"Perfect."

Barby and Jan came through the orchard and up on the porch. Barby was wearing an ornamental plastic head band, not too gaudy for daytime wear, but not too simple for anything dressy. She had arranged her hair so the gadget was hardly noticeable. A wave of smooth blond hair hid the little bump made by the battery.

"Technically," Barby stated, "it worked fine. But the program material was terrible."

The boys chuckled. "How do you know it was technically fine?" Scotty teased.

Barby looked at him coolly. "Because I heard Rick perfectly."

"And I heard you and Scotty," Rick agreed. "All three units work fine. Have you switched them off?"

THE COAST GUARD DRAWS A BLANK 121

Barby reached up and seemed to pat her hair slightly. "I forgot," she admitted. "Now it's off."

Rick looked at Jan. "Could you hear me through Barby's phone while I was talking?"

Jan shook her head. "No, I couldn't. I was listening, too. These are wonderful, Rick."

He smiled his thanks. "One interesting thing, though. I should have known, but it didn't occur to me. The receivers are directional."

"What's that?" Barby asked.

"Directional. The antenna is a tiny coil. When it's broadside to the incoming signal, the volume is loudest, but when it's end on, the volume is much less. So, if you can't hear well, just turn sideways. Turn until the signal is loudest."

Scotty took his transceiver from his pocket and examined it with pride. It was no larger than a pack of playing cards, and its sensitive microphone was incorporated right into the case. The tiny antenna was a piece of stiff steel wire only two inches long. The whole gadget fitted easily into an inside coat pocket without a noticeable bulge.

Barby's rig was slightly different. The antenna ran along one edge of the plastic strip. At one end the microphone was in contact with her head just above the ear, allowing for transmission of voice by bone conduction, a new method developed by the United States Air Force. At the other end of the band a tiny speaker made similar contact. Rick had worried about the effectiveness of both mike and phone, since he had never used the types before, but the design had turned out very well.

"Pretty neat if we do say so," Scotty admitted modestly.

"For once I agree with you," Barby said generously. "Now what, Rick? There isn't anything more to do, is there?"

"Not on these." But there was more to do along other lines. He was waiting for word from JANIG. Barby and Jan disappeared and returned in a few moments with iced drinks. The boys accepted them gratefully. It was a warm day.

"How about a swim?" Scotty suggested.

Rick was about to point out that they might have work to do when Joe Blake, the JANIG agent in charge at the laboratory, hailed him. Rick ran to meet the agent.

"The boys on the mainland didn't turn up a thing," Blake reported. "They searched from a half mile south of the pier to a half mile north. No pram anywhere."

Rick snapped his fingers. "I had a hunch they wouldn't! Okay. I'm going to take off right now and search the coast. If that pram wasn't connected with the attack on Duke and Jerry, I'll eat it."

"Good luck," Blake said. "Let me know if you need any help."

Rick hurried back to the porch. The JANIG scout team had reported early in the morning that the pram was gone from the pier. They had been cover-

THE COAST GUARD DRAWS A BLANK 123

ing the Whiteside area most of the night, searching for some sign of the pair that had attacked Rick's friends, but had turned up nothing suspicious.

Then, at Rick's suggestion, they had undertaken a search for the pram. His point was simply that he had never seen a pram in the Whiteside area—something that strangers would not have known. They might have figured that tying up in plain sight was the best way of hiding their boat. It would have been, if prams had been more common.

He motioned to Scotty. "Let's go. No sign of the pram."

Barby rose instantly. "Can we go with you?"

Rick considered, then nodded. He could see no objection to taking them on what could only be a short plane trip.

As they hurried to the plane, Scotty said, "What bothers me is, why didn't the JANIG team have someone at the landing?"

"They did," Rick replied. "I asked the same question. Their roving patrol had been by there a short time earlier, but saw nothing suspicious. After all, they can't post men everywhere. So two of them take turns keeping watch on the tidal flats, in case anyone tries to cross from the mainland directly to here. The other two keep moving."

"But it's funny anyone would attack Duke and Jerry," Barby objected. "It isn't . . . well, logical."

Rick grinned. Logic and his sister had never become well acquainted. He answered, "Suppose the enemy had been keeping track of movements by water to Spindrift? That isn't farfetched. They could do it easily without being noticed. Then, late yesterday, they saw two men get in a boat and come to the island. They were probably watching from cover. And what did they see?"

Jan answered excitedly, "Jerry, and a man who looked like my father!"

"That's it, Jan. So, if I guess correctly, they waited, hoping the man they thought was Dr. Morrison would come back. And he did, and they were waiting."

"Sounds reasonable," Scotty agreed. "Except for one small thing. Why attack Dr. Morrison when all they have to do is turn on a gadget and his mind goes blank?"

Jan shuddered visibly. Scotty added hurriedly, "Sorry, Jan."

"Maybe it's not that simple," Rick said thoughtfully. "If they only have to turn on a gadget, why did they need to drug Dr. Marks?"

There was no answer to that. As soon as they were air-borne, Rick headed north, searching the coastline, swinging low now and then to examine marinas where numbers of boats were tied up. Scotty kept the binoculars working, but there was no sign of a pram.

"Do you suppose it's under cover somewhere?" Barby asked.

Rick shrugged. "Maybe. They might cover it if

THE COAST GUARD DRAWS A BLANK 125

they thought anyone would come looking for it."

"They'll surely think of that, won't they?" Barby asked.

"Not necessarily. After all, they tied up at the pier in plain sight. I think they assumed no one would worry about a small rowboat. They just didn't know prams are uncommon."

Scotty put the glasses down for a moment and rubbed his eyes. "How far could they have come, anyway? We're miles above Spindrift, and no one would row that far."

He was right, of course. Rick admitted, "I've been racking my brains, and I can't remember whether or not the pram had an outboard motor. Just as I was about to take a close look, Jerry yelled. Do you remember, Scotty?"

Scotty shook his head. "But even with an outboard, they probably wouldn't have come this far."

"Check." Rick swung the Sky Wagon around and headed south on a straight course to Spindrift. As the fast little plane passed over the Brant house he throttled back and dropped lower. "Let's start the search again."

Every cove was investigated, and anything that might have been a boat was inspected carefully. Then, as they reached the summer colony north of Seaford, Barby exclaimed, "Look! There's that fancy houseboat again!"

The houseboat was putting out from land, swinging on a northerly course. Rick saw that it was powered by twin outboards and that it cruised at about fifteen knots.

Scotty yelled, "Hey! Behind the houseboat! Look at the dory they're towing!"

Rick swung low and craned his neck to see. It was! The houseboat used a pram as a tender, and the pram had its own low-power outboard motor.

"That's enough," he said with satisfaction. He kept the Sky Wagon on a southerly course until Seaford passed below, to keep the houseboaters from thinking the plane's sole interest had been in them. Beyond Seaford, he picked up Cap'n Mike's shack across the road from the old windmill.

"Let's see if Mike's home," he said, and stood the wagon up on a wing. He leveled off in time to buzz low over the old shack, which was not as shabby as it looked, and neat as a ship's cabin inside, then he pulled up into a screaming Immelman and looked out.

Cap'n Mike emerged from the shack waving what seemed to be a shirt. Rick waggled his wings in greeting, then did a wing over that brought him back low and fast over the old seaman's head. Cap'n Mike was grinning broadly as he waved.

Rick set a course north and slightly inland. In a short time he was back on the water again, taxiing to the Spindrift beach.

While the others went to the house, he stopped at the lab and reported to Joe Blake that he had found a pram. The agent got what details Rick had, and passed the word to the shore team on the mainland with instructions to follow the houseboat's movements from shore. Then he went to the phone and called Steve Ames.

Finally Joe hung up. "Steve says to keep an eye on the houseboat, but to take no action. He's going to do a little investigating."

"How?"

"He didn't say. But he expects to have something by tonight."

With that, Rick had to be satisfied.

Apparently Steve wasted no time, because Barby answered the phone just before dinner, then called:

"It's Steve Ames, Rick!"

Rick ran to the telephone.

"Thought I'd let you know," Steve reported. "I had the Coast Guard pay a visit to your houseboat this afternoon."

"You did?" Rick was incredulous. "But that means they're tipped off now that we're watching them!"

Steve sounded hurt. "Fine thing," he said, wounded. "No faith, huh? Ever hear of the Coast Guard's courtesy inspection service?"

"Sure. They'll inspect your boat for safety."

"That's it. And that's the gag we used. We sent a brand-new ensign, a real boyish type. He checked half a dozen boats before he got to the houseboat. When he pulled alongside and offered a courtesy investigation, they invited him aboard like an old friend."

"What did he find?" Rick asked excitedly.

"Nothing. All was in order, and the boat had plenty of extinguishers, life jackets, and other safety items, so he gave it a clean bill of health. They fed him iced tea and cookies, and waved good-by as if he was their long-lost son."

"What kind of people were they?"

"Two middle-aged couples. Business partners, from Trenton, and their wives. We got the names from him and checked. They really are partners, in a used-car business. Sorry, Rick. Looks like another dead end. The Coast Guard drew a blank this time."

"But there isn't another pram within miles of Spindrift," Rick objected.

"All right. We'll be keeping an eye on these people, but we have no grounds for any action. Any luck with the barber?"

"We haven't tried yet," Rick told him. "Tomorrow's the day. We've been getting the Megabuck network completed in case we need to communicate."

"Okay. Good luck, and keep me informed."

"I will, Steve."

Rick hung up and returned to the porch, deep in thought. To the waiting trio he said, "A blank. Nothing. Looks like the barber is still our best lead."

"That houseboat is in it, too," Barby stated positively.

"How do you know?" Scotty asked.

"It's too flashy," Barby explained. "Too bright. Really nice people wouldn't have a boat that color. You wait and see, they're in this somehow!"

Rick shook his head, more in sorrow than in anger. "Good thing the boat isn't bright red," he said wearily. "That would really be proof they're criminals!"

CHAPTER XIII

The Megabuck Mob Acts

BARBY BRANT flew up the stairs and ran down the hall, skidding to a stop in front of Rick's door. Then, conscious that her burst of speed was less than dignified, she drew herself up and tapped on the door gently.

Rick had just finished dressing. He opened the door, and his eyebrows went up at Barby's poorly concealed excitement.

"What's up?" he demanded. "Atom bomb ticking in the library or something?"

Barby made a heroic effort to be casual. "I just thought you might be interested. The houseboat is anchored in North Cove."

Rick was very much interested! North Cove was between Spindrift and Whiteside pier. He felt a tingle of excitement. Was the enemy closing in?

"Did you see it?" he asked.

"No, but Dad did. He went over to pick up the

morning papers, and there it was. It must have gone by during the night."

"Thanks, Barby," Rick said absently. His mind was already exploring the possibilities. The houseboat had taken up the ideal position for watching comings and goings from Spindrift. The cove was even close enough so the sound of the Sky Wagon's engine could be heard clearly.

Yet, according to Steve, the people on it were ordinary enough. There was nothing suspicious about them, except that they had the only pram in the area. He wondered if perhaps the pram had nothing to do with the attack on Duke and Jerry. After all, people on houseboats had to land once in a while, for shopping.

In the same moment, he realized that Whiteside was closed tight on Sunday evenings. There was nothing to be bought. That was when the attack had taken place.

He ate breakfast with minimum conversation, only vaguely conscious that the others were watching him with interest, aware that he was chewing over the problem in his own fashion.

After breakfast, Scotty broke in. "Well, what's all the high-brain activity leading up to?"

Rick was just about ready. "Couple of things," he said. "First, we have only two possibilities for enemy contacts in the area. The houseboaters, and the barber. There may be others, but we don't know about them."

"All right. What do we do about it?"

"Well, suppose both are involved. Is that a reasonable assumption?"

Scotty nodded thoughtfully. "I think so. The barber ties in because he came from Washington, and he has the machine. The houseboaters tie in because of the pram."

"Okay. Then if both are involved, they have to contact each other sometime. They have to exchange information, at the very least."

Scotty was with him. "And it would be easier for the houseboaters to contact the barber than vice versa. Because everyone has to get a haircut sooner or later. Right?"

"One hundred percent. So we keep a watch on both. I'll work it out with Joe Blake. We could keep watch by day, when possibility of contact is greatest because the barbershop is open. The JANIG team on the mainland can keep watch by night, because if the houseboaters and the barber meet at night it will have to be in the woods. Anywhere in town would be too obvious—except for the barbershop."

Barby and Jan had listened in silence, but Barby could contain herself no longer. "And we're going to help!"

To Barby's astonishment, Rick nodded. She had expected opposition. "You and Jan can keep watch of the houseboat. Scotty and I will take the mainland. If the houseboaters start for Whiteside pier, you'll tell us. We'll pick them up as they land and trail 'em."

Barby nodded, pleased. "The Megabuck Mob goes into action! We'll use the radio network. Right?"

"Yes. First thing is, where do you take up a position? If I remember correctly, you can see North Cove from the attic. It will be kind of hot up there, but maybe we can rig a fan."

"We won't mind," Jan said swiftly. "When do we start?"

"Right now."

Scotty spoke up. "You said you had a couple of things. What's the other one?"

"We have to get a look at the barber's machine. I don't know how we'll do it. But we can figure out something."

In the back of Rick's mind was the thought that the houseboaters might have moved nearer Whiteside for the purpose of contacting the barber, as well as to get a better look at traffic between Spindrift and the mainland. If that were true, they had better hurry.

He had another thought, too. "What time is it?"

Barby consulted her watch. "Five before eight. Why?"

"The barbershop doesn't open until nine. I think it might be useful to have someone call on the houseboaters and try to pump them a little. It might be interesting to hear why they chose to anchor in North Cove."

Barby's eyes got round. "Would you do it?"

Rick shook his head. "It can't be anyone from Spindrift, or from the police. It has to be someone plausible. I'm thinking of Cap'n Mike."

"Hey, that's just the ticket!" Scotty shook Rick's hand solemnly. "Cap'n Mike can pretend to be fishing, the way he used to when he was keeping an eye on Creek House. He could drift over to the houseboat and ask for a drink of water, or something, and strike up a conversation. They'd think he was just a typical salty character."

"Then that's how we'll do it. Scotty, suppose you get the binoculars for Barby, then rig up a fan. I'll go get Cap'n Mike. It won't take long, and we can have something set before the barbershop opens."

Scotty helped Rick push the plane out from the beach, then collected the binoculars. Rick warmed the plane and checked the gas. He could use a few minutes to gas up, too. There was a pier in Seaford where he could land and get the proper grade of fuel.

He taxied out, headed into the wind, and took off. Then, to confuse watchers, he headed straight for Whiteside. As he passed over the cove he saw the houseboat, anchored in the best position for watching the Spindrift–Whiteside boat course. His mouth was set in a straight line. Maybe there was no proof, but how much circumstantial evidence was needed to paint a picture? He was sure the houseboat was a part of the plot against the project.

Far inland, out of sight of the coast, he swung south, picked up Salt Creek and followed it to Smugglers' Reef. He turned down the coast past the town, buzzed Cap'n Mike's shack, and landed.

Captain Michael Aloysius Kevin O'Shannon was at the pier when he docked. Rick cut the engine and climbed out on the pontoon. He heaved a line to the old seaman, who hauled him to the pier.

Cap'n Mike was nearly seventy years old, but as Rick well knew, he had the vigor and keen mind of a man twenty years his junior. Under the battered master's cap was a thatch of white hair and a strong, weather-beaten face.

"About time you paid a friendly call," Cap'n Mike greeted him. "Sorry I found no strangers for you. Was goin' to call today. Where's Scotty?"

Rick felt a twinge of conscience. He had intended to pay a visit to his friend so many times, but something always seemed to get in the way. It had been many weeks since his last call.

"It isn't exactly a social call," he said apologetically. "We need your help, Cap'n Mike."

The old man looked at him quizzically. "What for? Fishin' or detectin'?"

"Detectin'," Rick answered.

"Accepted! Now I see why you were lookin' for strangers. When and where do I start?"

"Right now, at Spindrift. Can you come?"

"Wait'll I turn off my coffeepot. Anything I'll need?"

"We'll want you to do a little fishing, too."

Cap'n Mike nodded and hurried up the pier to his shack. In a few minutes he was back, rod case and tackle box in hand. He cast off and climbed into the plane. "Let's go, boy! Time's awastin'. Who we after this time?"

Rick started the engine and was air-borne before he answered. Then, almost immediately, he had to land again to take on gas. By the time he was in the air en route to Spindrift, Cap'n Mike was squirming so impatiently that the whole plane seemed to vibrate.

"Well, get on with it," he said irritably.

Rick smiled. "All right. We don't know who we're after."

Cap'n Mike grunted.

"Seriously, we don't. Some folks in a houseboat are anchored in North Cove. We want to find out why."

Cap'n Mike nodded sagely. "For no reason. They just might be dangerous criminals, so you want to investigate. All right, go ask 'em."

"We can't. We want you to go fishing, and work your way to the houseboat. Ask for a drink of water or something, then find out if you can what they're doing."

"Got it all worked out, have ye?" The old captain

Cap'n Mike quickly hauled the Sky Wagon to the pier

snorted. "Where's the fun in that? Like to do things my own way."

Rick hurriedly backtracked. "All right, do it anyway you like. We just want the information."

"What for?"

Rick sighed. "Can't tell you, Cap'n."

"Must be I got untrustworthy since I saw you last."

"It isn't that. It's a—well, it's a government matter."

Cap'n Mike smacked his thigh with a calloused hand. "I should 'a' known! All right, Rick. I'll do it. Then maybe I can get my congressman to tell me what I've done."

Rick made a great swing around Whiteside, pointing out the houseboat to Cap'n Mike as he passed North Cove, and landed off Pirate's Field. Scotty was waiting.

After greeting the old seaman, Scotty said, "The girls are watching from the attic. When do we get started?"

"As soon as Cap'n Mike is fixed up."

Cap'n Mike was pretty self-sufficient and required little attention. A cup of hot coffee, a jug of fresh water, a little bait and a rowboat, and he was on his way. Fortunately, the Spindrift boat landing was not in sight of North Cove. Cap'n Mike sculled slowly along the shore. He would emerge at the cove, surprising the houseboaters.

Rick checked on the girls. They were engaged in

making themselves comfortable on an old bed they had dragged in front of the window from which North Cove could be seen. He borrowed the glasses and looked at the houseboat, then handed them back, satisfied. They could see everything that went on.

Barby had her plastic set in place. Rick checked, and found that she had forgotten to turn it on. He grinned at her embarrassment.

"I'll call you from downstairs, and again when we get set on the mainland. Good luck."

The girls echoed the wish.

Cap'n Mike was fishing, allowing the rowboat to drift slowly in the direction of the cove. Rick watched awhile, and was satisfied. If anyone could put it over, Cap'n Mike could.

"Now," he asked Scotty, "how do we get to Whiteside without attracting attention?"

Scotty scratched his head. "I don't know. Unless you want to walk. We could cross the tidal flats and hike to town."

Rick vetoed that. "Too far and too slow. The barber would have time to cut twenty heads of hair before we got there."

"How about asking Jerry to come for us?"

"You've got it! He could come down the wood road and pick us up right behind the island. He knows the way." Rick went into the library and called the *Morning Record* number. Duke Barrows answered. Rick explained that they had to get to

Whiteside by the back way, without volunteering why. Duke hesitated, then agreed to send Jerry.

Rick smiled as he hung up. "Duke will get a story out of this somehow," he said. "He's so curious he could burst a seam. Come on. Jerry will get started right away."

Just before nine o'clock the boys and Jerry arrived at the newspaper office. Jerry was about to burst with curiosity, but he wasn't going to let it get the better of him. He hadn't asked a single question all the way from the wood road back of Whiteside into town.

Duke Barrows was apparently taking the same tack. He looked up as the boys entered, grunted, then continued working on the following day's editorial.

"Something just occurred to me," Rick said, after greeting the editor. "Isn't this pretty early for you and Jerry to be at work? I thought a morning paper didn't open for business until afternoon."

"We never sleep," Duke said, without interrupting his work. "What do you think this is, *The New York Times?*"

"Never occurred to me," Rick said politely. "Although the quality of the paper is about the same."

The editor looked at Jerry. "When he talks like that, he wants something. What is it?"

"Search me. I don't know what these two want, and I don't know when they got deaf. Notice they're both wearing hearing aids?"

Duke hadn't. The boys grinned at his look of astonishment.

"What we'd like," Scotty said, "if you care to cooperate, is to have someone take a look at the barbershop. We want to know if the new barber is on the job."

Duke sharpened his pencil with loving care, using a penknife. "I won't ask why you can't take a look yourselves," he said finally. "It's pretty obvious."

"Not to me," Jerry objected.

"It should be. They don't want the barber to get a look at them, because he saw them in Washington. They don't want him to know they're interested, or that they know he's in town."

Rick started to ask how Duke had known that much, then realized that the editor had simply drawn the correct conclusion from the few words that had been said before. Again Rick gained a clear insight into how a little information can be built up into a lot. No wonder Steve and his people had so much trouble protecting official secrets.

Duke put his pencil down and rose. "It happens that I need a haircut. Stand by." At the door he paused. "Anything else you want to know?"

"We want to know about his massage machine," Rick said urgently. "Find out all you can, Duke. Please? Particularly if it has any electrical connections besides the wall plug."

Duke studied them thoughtfully for a long moment, then turned and left.

Jerry watched his boss leave. "He's kinder to you two than I would be," he stated. "He didn't ask a single question, even about the hearing aids."

Rick considered. There was nothing secret about the Megabuck network, except that he and Barby would use it for a mind-reading act. Jerry was trustworthy; he wouldn't give the act away.

"Promise you'll keep it to yourself," Rick asked, and at Jerry's excited nod he took the tiny receiver from his ear and handed it to Jerry.

The reporter held it to his own ear, moving closer to Rick because the cord was just long enough to reach from ear to inner pocket.

Rick said, "Barby, say hello to Jerry."

Apparently Barby did, because Jerry gave a surprised start.

"Can I talk to her?" Jerry asked.

Barby answered the question herself. The microphone, built right into the little unit, was very sensitive and Rick's thin jacket did not muffle it very much.

"I'm fine," Jerry said.

Rick grinned.

Scotty could hear both sides of the conversation through his own set. Now he broke in. "Any sign of activity yet?"

"Cap'n Mike is fishing right near the houseboat. I can see the people on the houseboat, but they're just having breakfast on the rear deck. Where are you?"

"In the newspaper office. Duke has gone to check on the barber."

Rick held out his hand and Jerry gave him the earpiece, grinning. "What a rig!" the reporter marveled. "Where did you get it?"

"Built it."

During the next half hour, while they waited for Duke to return, Rick told Jerry the story of the Megabuck Mob, omitting only what followed when Steve Ames arrived.

Then Duke returned, freshly barbered, trying to scratch his back. "One thing about this new barber," he greeted them. "He's no better at keeping hair out of your shirt than Vince is. Why is it that barbers can't cut hair without getting it into places where it itches?"

Rick smiled sympathetically. He knew how it was. No matter how careful a barber tried to be, it seemed impossible to get a haircut without a shower of hair clippings down the back. Usually they lodged where it was impossible to scratch.

Duke rubbed against the doorframe. "It's Vince Lardner's day off," he began.

Rick tensed. If the houseboaters were going to contact the barber, they would naturally try to choose a time when they could see him alone. Maybe there had been an earlier contact, and the barber had told them he would be alone today. That might account for the houseboat's moving closer to Whiteside.

"Vince had gone fishing." The editor grinned. "I suspect that's the only reason he got a helper, anyway, so he could go fishing more often. There isn't really enough work in town for more than one barber."

"Did you look at the massage machine?" Rick asked anxiously.

The editor nodded. "It's nothing but a hood, with three ordinary massage gadgets inside. Vibrator heads, I think they're called."

That tallied with the description Steve's agent had given. "Did you examine it closely?" Rick pursued.

"Yes. There's only one cord attached—the power cord. But I did notice an interesting thing. Set around the edges are little disks, like round covers. I started to lift one up, but the barber asked me to stop. He said the machine is adjusted very carefully and I might upset the adjustment."

"Tough luck," Scotty said, disappointed.

"Oh, I don't know." Duke's eyes twinkled. "I got enough of a look to see two tiny holes in the piece of stuff the disk covered. The stuff was black, probably plastic. Like telephones are made of."

"In other words," Rick said slowly, "you saw holes for electrical plugs?"

"I think so. I don't know what else they could be."

Rick and Scotty exchanged glances.

"What does it mean?" Jerry asked.

Rick answered. "We don't know. And I'm not kidding. We really don't know."

"I believe you," Duke said briefly. "Okay. I've done my bit, including getting my hair cut. Anything else?"

"We'd like to stick around," Rick replied. "Jerry already knows about this, but Barby is watching a houseboat anchored in North Cove. If anyone leaves the houseboat for the Whiteside pier, she'll call us. We'll take over at the pier. It just might happen that the houseboater will pay a call on the barber."

Duke didn't comment, but Rick knew the editor's mind was at work. "Make yourself at home," Duke said, and went back to his editorial writing.

Now and then Barby called, wanting to chat, but Rick discouraged her. He was reasonably sure the enemy wouldn't be listening in on the extremely short wave length on which the Megabuck network operated, but there was no use taking any chances. After each conversation he identified the sets with his own amateur call letters, even though it was unlikely anyone could hear the conversation. The little sets operated essentially on a line of sight because of the short wave length used. They couldn't be heard beyond the horizon, if they were heard that far.

After an hour of waiting, Barby called in high excitement. Cap'n Mike was aboard the houseboat! The boys waited anxiously for some further report, but Barby was only able to say that the old seaman had departed after a ten-minute visit and was now fishing again.

At noon Jerry and Scotty slipped out for a sandwich. When they returned, Rick and Duke went to eat. According to Barby, all was quiet.

Around one o'clock Cap'n Mike returned to Spindrift and reported a friendly conversation with the houseboaters. They had anchored in North Cove because someone down the coast had told them fishing was good around there, which was a true statement.

The retired skipper had only one additional comment, which Barby relayed. The folks had been friendly, but he thought they were a little nervous, and anxious to get rid of him. He had no other information of value.

At midafternoon Jerry went on a brief sortie, came back, and reported business was slow in the barbershop, which was not unusual for a Tuesday. The barber was reading a magazine.

Rick and Scotty were restless. The chairs in the newspaper office were hard, and they had exhausted the reference materials on the bookshelf.

Duke Barrows looked up from a story he was editing and grinned. "Espionage isn't as adventurous as some folks would like you to believe. It's generally nothing but sitting. And waiting. Just as you're doing now."

Rick grinned back. Duke was telling him nothing he didn't know. He had waited like this before.

Barby called urgently, "Rick! The pram is leaving. One man in it, and he's just starting the outboard motor!"

"All right," he said swiftly. "Let us know which way he goes."

In a moment Barby answered. "He's going to the pier!"

"Roger. We're moving!"

CHAPTER XIV

Surveillance—with Cereal

THE plan of action had been set in advance. Scotty hurried out, while Rick settled down to wait. Scotty, using Jerry's car, would locate the houseboater at the pier. Rick would stand by, ready to take over as necessary.

A short time later Scotty called on the Megabuck network. "I'm in the pier parking lot. He's tying the pram up."

"Can he see you?"

"Not unless he comes over and inspects the cars."

"Okay."

After a few minutes, Scotty reported again. "He's hiking in the direction of Whiteside. Thumb out. He wants a ride."

"Don't give him one," Barby interjected urgently. "He might recognize you."

"He's hitchhiking," Scotty explained. "He doesn't even know I exist."

"What are his chances?" Rick asked.

"Good. There's a fair amount of traffic."

Rick waited, alert for Scotty's next report. It came almost immediately. "I'm moving. A truck picked him up. Stand by."

Then soon afterward, "We're coming into the outskirts of town."

Rick walked from the newspaper office to the sidewalk and leaned casually against the building, eyes on the direction from which the quarry and Scotty would come. He felt just fine. The little network was taking all the strain out of shadowing. He thought of the many times when such communications would have come in very handy indeed.

"Moving down Main Street," Scotty reported. "Watch it!"

Rick saw a truck come into sight and slow as it neared the barbershop. A man got out, thanked the driver, then stood looking around. He spotted the barbershop, but instead of going in, he went to the window of the Sports Center and stood quietly, ostensibly inspecting equipment. Rick decided he was just looking the street over before making contact.

"I'm on him," he said quietly for Scotty's benefit. "He's casing the street. He'll probably go into the barbershop any minute now."

Scotty drove down the main street, and as he passed the barbershop, he reported, "There's a man in the chair. Maybe our friend is waiting for him to leave."

"We'll see."

Rick's plans had not gone beyond this point. The objective had been to see whether the houseboaters made contact with the barber. But now he realized that a simple contact wasn't proof of anything. Who was to say that the houseboater hadn't really wanted a haircut?

If only there were some way of overhearing the conversation . . .

Jerry Webster came out and stood beside him. "See your man?"

Rick gestured. "In front of the Sports Center."

"What are you going to do now?"

"I was just wondering the same thing."

Jerry grinned. "Don't tell me you don't have a complete plan! Why, I thought by now you'd have the barbershop wired for sound."

Rick stared at him. Wired! Why not? And it wasn't too late, if Jerry would help.

"Will you do something more for me?"

Jerry looked martyred. "Might as well. I'm in this up to my neck, anyway."

Scotty joined them. He had parked the car around the corner. "What's happening?"

"Just had a brain storm," Rick told him. He explained rapidly, and the two started to chuckle.

"It should work," Scotty agreed. "Go ahead. I'll take over the watch. Hey! There he goes."

The houseboater had just walked into the barbershop.

Rick ran to the next corner and into the grocery store. He hesitated briefly, then picked out two boxes of cereal, and added a box of sugar. He had them put into a bag, paid for them, and hurried back.

Inside the newspaper office, he took out his scout knife and carefully slit the top of one cereal box. He removed the little radio from his pocket, unplugged the earphone, and put the radio on top of the cereal. He borrowed cellophane tape and taped the box shut, then he put both boxes of cereal back in the bag with the sugar on top.

He handed the bag to Jerry. "Do your stuff."

Jerry took it and hurried out the door. Rick and Scotty watched as he went up the street and turned in at the barbershop.

Scotty shook his head. "All I can hear in the earphone is a crackling noise."

"Probably the paper bag," Rick said. "It would crackle as he walks."

They waited impatiently. Presently Jerry emerged without the bag and walked down the street to join them.

"The man in the chair is about done," he reported. "The one you're after is reading a magazine. I said I'd be back in a few minutes, left the bag, and walked out."

"There's the other customer now," Rick said. A man had just emerged from the barbershop and was going up the street in the opposite direction. "Good!

They'll talk fast now, because they'll be afraid you'll come back."

"I still hear the crackling noise," Scotty objected. "Someone's talking in the background, but I can't hear it because of the snapping and popping."

Rick swallowed hard. Was something wrong? "Let's see." He borrowed Scotty's earpiece and held it to his own ear. For a second he listened, horrified. It sounded like the Battle of Bull Run!

Barby broke in faintly through the noise. "Rick! I've been listening. What's that noise?"

He explained quickly. "We planted one unit in a box of cereal and Jerry put it in the barbershop."

Barby gasped. "In a box of cereal? What kind?"

"Crummies. Your favorite."

"Oh, Rick!" The girl's voice rose to a wail. "Don't you remember the commercial? Crisp, crackly Crummies! The cereal that sings for your breakfast!"

He got it, then. "Okay, Barby." To the others, he said unhappily, "Well, it was a great idea. Only I forgot one thing. I didn't pick a quiet breakfast food. That noise is the radio settling through the Crummies—the loudest cereal on the market."

The three looked at each other helplessly. There wasn't a thing that could be done about it.

"Noisy breakfast food," Scotty said unbelievingly.

Jerry promised, "I'll never eat it again!" The reporter straightened his coat and tie and gave his hatbrim a jaunty flick. "Well, here I go for my haircut. Might as well do something constructive."

The crackling, popping, snapping continued unabated. "Listen to it," Rick said hopelessly.

Three quarters of an hour later, when Jerry brought the bag back, the Crummies were still crackling happily. Not a word of conversation had been overheard.

CHAPTER XV

A Matter of Brain Waves

BARBY, Jan, and Scotty were kind to Rick, which annoyed him considerably. If they had scolded him for bad judgment, called him a chucklehead, or even ignored him, it would have been all right. But they all had to reassure him and tell him it could have happened to anyone, and so on, and on. All of which made it unbearable.

He was more sure than ever that the houseboaters and barber were connected, but he still had no clear evidence. Of course he had made a report of the day's activities to Steve, who at least hadn't tried to be nice about it.

"An agent can't always think of everything," was Steve's comment. "But he can try. Sometimes, when he fails to take a factor into consideration, he gets away with it. Sometimes he fails. Sometimes he ends up dead, because of his poor judgment. Be glad your lives weren't hanging in the balance."

Rick took the lesson to heart. He wouldn't make the same mistake twice.

On the evening of the cereal fiasco, Parnell Winston returned to Spindrift after another visit to Dr. Chavez. He called Steve Ames and spent a long time talking to the JANIG agent. Then he called the project team and the boys into the library.

"We're on the track of something," he reported. "At least we think we are. It's so incredible that I simply can't believe it. If true, it means some unfriendly nation is so far ahead of us scientifically that we should all be trembling in our boots."

Rick had realized that only agents of a hostile country could be involved in the actions against the project team. Everyone present had known as much, without a word being spoken. Only another country could gain from disruption of the project.

"Chavez and I have run a series of EEG's on Marks. We now have the records of EEG's on the other two team members, and Steve has managed to turn up a pre-project EEG on one which gives us a basis of comparison. Now, to comprehend our tentative hypothesis, you must understand something of what is known about the brain."

Rick prepared to listen without much understanding. The field in which Parnell Winston worked was new and strange to him, and while he understood some of the basic theories, he got lost when Winston got highly technical.

"Our understanding of the human brain is fairly

recent," Winston began, "and we're still only on the threshold of knowledge. In a way, we've just discovered the tools of research. The principal tool, of course, is electricity. Through it we can explore the electrochemical nature of brain processes."

Rick was with him so far. He concentrated hard, not wanting to miss a word.

"There's no point in reviewing the entire history of brain physiology. You all know of Pavlov's work on conditioned reflexes. And you all know that Fritsch and Hitzig demonstrated that, when electrically stimulated, certain portions of the brain show a response. You also know that Caton discovered many years ago that the brain itself produces electric currents."

Rick didn't know, but he intended to find out. There must be some works on brain physiology in the library.

"However, the important modern work started with Berger in the late 1920's. He found that the brain emits a definite pulse of activity, which was then known as the 'Berger rhythm.'

"Since then, Berger's work has been very much refined. We now know that the brain actually produces a number of clearly defined electrical rhythms. These rhythms have been used in medical diagnosis of brain injury. Walter, in England, has even developed a machine that will show whether or not people will get along with each other, by analysis of their wave patterns."

This was interesting, and Rick intended to find out more about it. But he began to wish Winston would come to the point.

"I might add that the rhythmic brain patterns seem to be highly individual. No two are alike, even in identical twins. However, each person shows a pattern that remains fairly constant, even over a period of years.

"With this background, you will understand when I report that the EEG's taken of our colleagues brains are completely abnormal. The EEG's were taken while they were awake. Yet, the most prominent pattern is the delta rhythm that is universally associated with sleep and some types of damage to the brain."

"Are there any other signs of physical damage?" Hartson Brant asked.

"No. All tests are negative. Spinal taps show no concussion, and there is no evidence of trauma of any kind other than psychic. Yet, the delta rhythms persist. In the one case where we have an EEG taken before the—incidents, let's call them—the pattern is entirely different. The scientist had a pattern of a well-known type which bears no resemblance to the EEG taken after the incident."

Dr. Morrison leaned forward. "What is your conclusion?"

"That our mysterious enemy has somehow caused damage of an unknown kind, by remote means. And that can mean only one thing: The damage was caused electronically, probably by transmission through the air."

"Incredible," Weiss muttered, and the sentiment was reflected in the astonished gasps of the others.

"Let's consider the implications of Parnell's statement," Hartson Brant said slowly. "If he is correct, then the enemy has devised a means for causing brain disruption in an individual. A transmitted signal would inevitably strike countless others; there can be no such thing as a beam of radiation that strikes one person at a distance while missing all others. Therefore, this beam must affect only one person among many."

"But how can a beam be tuned to one person?" Rick asked.

"I don't know, Rick." Hartson Brant turned to Winston. "Do you?"

"No. I have only a hypothesis, and one so far afield from what we know of the brain today that I even hesitate to suggest it. Let me ask a question. If the enemy could have access to the brain pattern of an individual—and remember such patterns are no more similar than fingerprints—could the enemy then transmit a signal that would affect only that pattern?"

Julius Weiss objected. "The supposition is based on scientific knowledge that does not exist."

"So far as we know," Dr. Morrison added.

Parnell Winston held up his hands. "I'm as aware as any of you that the hypothesis assumes a knowledge of the brain that is incredibly far advanced. But let us consider the evidence. The three scientists who have fallen victim show the same signs of brain damage. Investigation indicates that they were different types who probably had dissimilar patterns. We also have the special case of Dr. Marks, who was drugged while on the train. The person who drugged him dropped soluble salt paste on the rug of his room. Can we accept the fact that the salt paste was used for EEG electrodes, and a recording made while Marks was under the influence of the drug? We can't prove it, but what other explanation can there be?"

Dr. Morrison shook his head. "Suppose we accept that theory. How does that account for the other two? They were under guard, and there is no evidence that they ever were drugged. If we accept your hypothesis, we must also accept the theory that the other two men somehow were given an EEG examination and their patterns recorded."

An idea was growing in Rick's mind. Suddenly he blurted, "That's where the barber comes in!"

"The barber's machine was examined by Steve's men and found harmless," Hartson Brant pointed out.

Scotty spoke up quickly. "Yes, but when Duke looked at it this morning, he found electrical connections! Why couldn't an EEG be taken with such a gadget?"

Parnell Winston considered. "It could," he said finally. "I would need to examine the machine, but in theory any gadget that fits over the head could be adapted for proper placement of electrodes. The recorder would be difficult to hide, however, unless it was in another room."

Rick sank back and looked at Scotty. No wonder the barber had wanted to give a treatment to Hartson Brant. The elevator operator's wink had told him that the scientist had been on the fourth floor, where the project team was located.

"Didn't you ever have your hair cut in the arcade shop, Dr. Morrison?" Rick asked.

"No, Rick. I used a barber in a hotel nearby, one I've patronized for years."

"But the other two did use the shop in the building," Scotty finished, "and Dr. Marks had no need for a barber, so they had to get at him some other way!"

"It seems reasonable," Hartson Brant admitted. "The pieces fall into place nicely. But we must first accept Parnell's theory that some kind of pattern can be transmitted that will interfere with normal brain activity. If we believe it, we must also believe that the enemy is so far ahead of us in brain physiology that we are hopelessly outdistanced. I can't believe so much progress could have taken place without some word of it leaking out."

Parnell Winston shrugged. "It seems incredible, Hartson. But we haven't another theory, much less a better one."

"We had better make sure no one takes EEG's of the rest of us, in any case," Weiss suggested dryly.

Rick added, "And don't get any haircuts until this is all straightened out!"

When the meeting broke up, Rick and Scotty walked to the front porch where the girls were listening to the music of a Newark disk jockey on Barby's portable radio.

"Lot of puzzled people in this neighborhood," Rick said. "Including me."

"And me," Scotty agreed. "And I'll bet I know the most curious one of all."

"Who?"

"Cap'n Mike."

Rick grinned. At least the rest of them had some information. Even Duke and Jerry had enough to know that national security was somehow involved. But the captain, who had the liveliest curiosity of all, knew the least.

As Rick dropped him off in front of the old windmill, Cap'n Mike had grunted, "When you can trust me a little more, you might tell me what this was all about."

Actually, Cap'n Mike's visit to the houseboat hadn't been particularly productive. He had little to add to the Coast Guard inspector's description, aside from his feeling that the houseboaters had wanted to get rid of him.

Scotty asked, "Why would anyone want to disrupt the brains of the project team? Seems to me that's doing it the hard way. Assassination would be a lot easier."

Rick shook his head. He had wondered about the same thing.

Barby and Jan motioned for silence. They were listening to a vocalist who happened to be Barby's favorite of the moment.

The boys stood silent for a few minutes; then, by unspoken agreement, turned and went back into the house.

Hartson Brant came down the stairs, dressed in a suit, with white shirt and tie. Rick stared at him. "Going somewhere, Dad?"

"Yes. Parnell Winston has disturbed me deeply, with the implications of his theory. I'm going to pay a call on an old friend in Newark, an associate of Chavez. I want to explore some of the electrophysiological background of his hypothesis. I won't be very late. Is there any gas in the car?"

"Almost full," Scotty said.

The boys went on upstairs into their adjoining rooms. For a few minutes Rick tinkered with his camera equipment, then he went back down to the library and searched the shelves for something to read. He finally settled on W. Grey Walter's *The Living Brain* and carried it back up to his room.

He sat down in the old leather armchair and manipulated buttons on one arm. The light brightened to reading intensity, and the back tilted to the most comfortable position. He had wired the chair himself, and it fit him perfectly. He settled down to read.

Time passed as he lost himself in the clear, exciting descriptions in Dr. Walter's book. He heard a bell ring downstairs, but paid no attention. Then Scotty stuck his head in the door. "Rick! Your mother's calling you."

Rick sat up swiftly. It was true, and his mother had urgency in her voice.

He dropped the book and ran to the stairs, going down them three at a time. A strange, dark-haired man was standing in the hallway, and his mother, Barby, and Jan were waiting for him with strained white faces.

"Your father has been hurt," Mrs. Brant said with false calm. "He's on this gentleman's houseboat!"

CHAPTER XVI

The Vanishing Mermaids

Parnell Winston worked as Hartson Brant described his experience.

"There really isn't much to it," Mr. Brant said. "I started out for Whiteside in the fast boat."

Winston focused a flashlight into one eye, then the other.

"I was on the north side of North Cove when the boat smashed into something. I was thrown violently into the water."

Winston tested the scientist's reflexes, using a finger instead of the traditional rubber hammer.

"Apparently I was badly shaken up, because my memory becomes unclear at this point. I do recall being fished out of the water, and when I came to enough to recognize my surroundings, I was in a strange room. It turned out to be the cabin of the houseboat."

"Do you remember any strange sensations, or smells?" Winston asked.

Rick listened, his heart pounding.

"None. The people on the houseboat were most considerate. One of the men insisted that I get into some of his spare clothes, and I did so. One of the women—the wife of the man who came here, I believe—made me a cup of hot consommé. They told me I was apparently whole, no broken bones."

"They were very pleasant and helpful," Rick admitted.

The houseboaters had done just the right things, including coming to Spindrift for help rather than bringing the scientist home in the slow-moving and rather uncomfortable pram. Instead, Hartson Brant had waited on the houseboat while one of the men brought the pram to the island with a request that someone follow him back in a more comfortable boat.

Rick and Scotty had done so, and were almost limp with relief at finding the scientist apparently unhurt and comfortable.

"How does your head feel?" Parnell Winston demanded.

"Rather stuffy," the scientist admitted. "I'm finding it difficult to collect my thoughts. Parnell, why all these questions?"

The cyberneticist rubbed his bushy eyebrows with both hands, a habit he had when agitated. "Hartson, as you know, I am not a doctor of medicine. However, I do claim competence as a physiologist, and consequently bodily reactions are familiar to me. I believe you have been drugged."

"Drugged?" Rick's heart stopped momentarily.

"Yes. I've looked for the mark of a hypodermic needle, but there is none. If I'm correct, the drug was a light one, possibly amytal. Your reflexes are slower than normal, even taking the accident and subsequent shock into account, and your pupils react slowly."

Rick came to a sudden decision. He went to the desk and picked up the phone.

"What are you doing?" Hartson Brant demanded.

"I'm calling Steve Ames. We need help."

In a few minutes Rick had the agent on the wire and was giving him the details of the accident over the scrambler system. He concluded, "If Dad was drugged by the houseboaters, as Dr. Winston thinks, that means the enemy has his brain pattern!"

Steve Ames asked, "Is Winston there?"

"Yes."

"Ask him a question for me. Would the brain waves be considered quasi-optical?"

Steve meant would the waves be of such high frequency that they would act like light. Rick put the question to Winston.

"Tell Steve the answer is a qualified yes."

Rick repeated the information.

"All right. Then we must assume that the brain scrambler—or whatever you call it—can operate only from short distances, approximately to the horizon. Tell your father he is to get out of town. Have him pack a bag, then deliver him to the New York JANIG office. We'll take it from there. Got it?"

Rick had it. "How do I make sure we're not followed?"

Steve paused. "That's a tough one. Air travel would be surest. Do you have any landing lights on Spindrift?"

"No. Besides, it's a short runway, and only a pilot who knew the island could possibly land at night."

"I've got a pilot who knows it, so forget going to New York. Rig lights of some kind. You can put lights on the roof of the lab building, I'm sure. Then put a pair of lights at each side of the runway's end, so he'll know how far he can go. If you have nothing else, soak newspapers in gasoline. He'll buzz the island. That will be your signal to light up."

"Is Mike Malone the pilot?" Malone had landed there before.

"Yes. He'll take over. Just deliver your father intact."

"If we can," Rick said slowly. "Steve, suppose the enemy activates their machine when they hear the plane? Suppose they suspect he's getting away and turn on the mind reader?"

"We'll have to chance it. Best thing is to move fast. Get your father in with Mike, and let them clear out. I'll tell Mike to put distance between him and you as fast as he can."

"All right, Steve." There seemed to be no other way.

Rick turned to his father and Winston, and repeated the conversation.

"He's right, Hartson," Winston said. "You're in good enough shape to travel. Better get packed." The cyberneticist looked at Rick. "What did you call the enemy gadget? A mind reader? That's an odd name."

"I didn't think about it," Rick told him. "The name just popped into my mind. But doesn't the enemy machine read the patterns in peoples' minds, then erase them?"

"As good a name as any, I guess," Winston agreed. "Well, let's tell the others. Then you have work to do getting ready for the plane, Rick."

Mrs. Brant, after making sure that her husband was no more than slightly dazed, had been forced to turn her attention to Barby and Jan. The two girls were on the verge of sheer hysteria with fear for their fathers. Scotty had joined Mrs. Brant, in an effort to soothe the girls frayed nerves. Now, as Rick opened the library door, he could see that the two pretty young faces were tear-streaked, but as calm as could be expected under the circumstances. Scotty looked worn out. Rick could only marvel at his mother. She could always be relied upon in a crisis.

Mrs. Brant listened to her son's report, then

nodded firmly. "Steve is wise to insist, Rick. I'll help your father pack."

Rick beckoned to Scotty. "We have work to do. Let's start with the lab."

On the way, he filled Scotty in on the details of what had happened in the library. Then he asked, "How did you get the girls calmed down?"

Scotty shook his head wearily. "It wasn't fun. The poor kids are scared stiff. Remember they haven't been exposed to stuff as we have. To them, our stories are just exciting fun, because we leave out the rough parts. Now they're getting a taste of this business the way it really is."

"Did you say that?"

"That, and a thousand other things. Nothing did much good, and Mom couldn't make any headway, either. Another ten minutes of tears and the island would have been under water, honest. Finally I got rough. I told them we were all in this, and they were only creating a nuisance that complicated things and didn't help at all. Then Mom chimed in. You know how she does. Never raises her voice. She said real courage consisted of being terribly frightened, but trying to remain calm in spite of it. Then she said she was rapidly becoming ashamed of both of them. That did it. They stuck their chins in the air, wiped off the tears, and actually managed a smile."

"Good for them!" Rick exclaimed.

Inside the laboratory they went at once to the

stockroom. Floodlights were stored there, among other items. Extension cords were plentiful, and there were electric outlets on the roof. In a few moments the boys had strung the lights and Rick had readjusted the board downstairs, so that all the lights were on a single circuit. That way, they could all be switched on or off at once.

Joe Blake came to watch. Rick explained what he was doing, and told Joe of Steve's conversation.

"I know," Joe said. "Steve called me on the radio. He didn't want us shooting Mike down for trying to land without warning. But how come you can cut circuits in and out like this?"

"We never know when an experiment will call for electric power in some unexpected place," Rick explained. "The main board is set up so we can do just about anything we need to. We can feed normal current in, or 440 volts, and we can cross-link the circuits any way we like."

Scotty checked Rick's work, then took the switch handle. He touched the contacts briefly, and there was a quick pulse of light as the roof lighted up and went dark again.

"I'll stand by here," Scotty said. "You stand by at the end of the runway. Are we going to use gasoline?"

"We'll have to. It would take a while to run power from the house and hook up lighting units. Gasoline will be quicker and easier. Let's go."

There was a supply of gasoline for the boats. Rick

THE VANISHING MERMAIDS 171

got a five-gallon can while Scotty collected newspapers. Two trash cans served as containers. The cans were filled with newspapers, then drenched in gasoline and placed at the last possible point of runway that could be used. If Mike overshot the containers he would land in the sea.

Rick worried about the problem of lighting the containers without getting burned, then went to the workshop and selected rags. He twisted the rags loosely and tied them together, poured gasoline into a bucket and soaked his rag fuse. The last step was to insert one end of the fuse in each can. When the time came, he would be between the cans, and he would light the center of the rag string. The fire would travel rapidly, because of the gasoline.

In case Mike was delayed for any great period, Rick kept the gasoline handy. He might have to wet down the cans and fuse again. He had forgotten to ask where Mike would come from, and Steve hadn't volunteered. Probably he would come from Washington, which meant about an hour's flying time in the plane Mike would use, a fast little four-place job that Rick had long coveted. But Mike wouldn't be ready for take-off instantly. Time had to be allowed for Steve to give him instructions, to get from wherever he was to the airport, and then get the plane gassed and ready. Allow another hour. That meant two hours in all.

Inside, Rick was still scared. How did they know the electronic mind reader wouldn't be activated at any moment? He hurried into the house and went upstairs to where his father was packing. He couldn't do anything, and he knew it. But it helped, just being near the scientist. Apparently Scotty felt the same. He had joined Hartson Brant, too. But Barby, Jan, and Mrs. Brant had preceded him.

The scientist smiled. "Never had so much help packing before."

The smile was strained, and Rick thought he knew why. He had seen his father face great physical danger without losing a bit of his composure. But the insidious weapon that could read all reason out of minds was far more horrible to a man like Hartson Brant than any physical danger could be. Bullets, knives, and clubs may leave bad wounds, or they may kill. But what chance is there for anyone with a damaged brain?

Scotty looked at his watch and held it up for Rick to see. Nearly an hour and three-quarters had passed since the call to Steve. Rick gestured to Scotty and urged, "Hurry, Dad."

"I'm ready." The scientist closed his bag. Barby got to it first and lugged it down the stairs, refusing Scotty's offer of help.

The boys went to their stations while the others waited on the porch. Rick checked to be sure he had matches, then worried because a wind had sprung up. Suppose it blew his match out? He was about to go borrow his father's lighter when he heard the far-off drone of a plane. There wasn't time now! He held the matches in his hand, ready.

The drone grew nearer, rising to a high whine. The plane was diving! Suddenly it was overhead and gone with a crash of sound. Rick saw its lights head out to sea. Mike was making a tight turn to come in for a landing.

Rick's lips formed the words. "Now, Scotty! Now!"

And, as though he had heard, Scotty threw the switch. Lights flared on the lab roof, outlining it clearly. Rick struck a match and held it to the saturated cord of rags. Flaming gasoline ran along the cord in both directions, ran up the sides of the cans. There was a loud whoosh of exploding gasoline, and both cans were ablaze. Rick ran away from the heat.

Mike came in low and fast over the lab roof and slapped the plane down on the turf. In a moment he applied the brakes and the wheels whined their protest as they dug up grass. Then the plane was rolling to a stop directly in front of the house.

The pilot jumped out and called, "Hello, gang! Come on, sir. No time to waste!"

Hartson Brant kissed Mrs. Brant and the girls, found time to pat Rick's shoulder, and climbed in. Rick took the suitcase from Barby and handed it to the scientist. The door closed and the plane was whirling, catching them in its prop blast. Mike taxied back fast to the laboratory, turned the plane and revved up, holding on the brakes. Rick saw Scotty emerge from the lab building and go right back in again as the prop wash caught him. Then the plane was rolling . . . and lifting. Mike skimmed low over the burning trash cans, banked out to sea, and was gone.

Rick felt a sob rising in his throat and resolutely squelched it. He walked to the burning cans and dropped covers on them. Scotty cut the lights on the lab building.

Had they made it? They wouldn't know. Not until Steve reported that the scientist was safe.

On the porch, Barby asked, "How soon will we know?"

Rick was proud of her. Her voice had trembled only slightly. "Probably not until tomorrow, Sis. Come on. Let's all hike off to bed. It's been a rough evening."

"All right. Rick, we still don't know for sure, do we? About the people in the houseboat?"

"Not for sure. But we have a pretty good idea. How else would Dad get drugged?"

"Mightn't they have given him a sedative?" Jan asked. "That would have the same effect."

Rick hadn't thought of that. He admitted it was possible.

"I wish the radio trick had worked," Barby said sadly. "I wish we had some way of getting a radio on the houseboat. Then we could listen in on everything they said."

"No way of doing it," Rick said. He was very tired.

"Forget it for now and let's all turn in. We can talk some more in the morning."

Steve Ames phoned at five o'clock in the morning. Rick had been sleeping lightly, his rest broken by nightmares that he couldn't remember when he awoke. He got to the phone in the hall. "Just a minute," he said. "Let me get downstairs to the switch."

The entire family was close on his heels as he went into the library. He threw the scrambler switch, then asked anxiously, "Yes, Steve?"

"Just had word, Rick, so I called in spite of the hour. Your father is safe inside the compound at Los Alamos. He's all right. And just as a precaution, he'll spend most of his time in a shielded area where no radio signal can penetrate. Now go on back to bed and get some sleep."

Rick thanked him gratefully. Los Alamos! That was one of the two main atomic energy weapons laboratories. No place in the United States was more closely guarded. Now he could be sure his father was safe as anyone could be.

He repeated the conversation to his anxious family. "Now," he said, echoing Steve's advice, "let's get back to bed. Perhaps we can really sleep for a change."

He did sleep. It was nearly noon before he awoke. He got up sleepily and found Scotty had just barely preceded him and was now taking a shower.

Downstairs, things were apparently normal. Mrs.

Brant and Mrs. Morrison were at work on lunch, but since an hour was too long to wait, Rick had a bowl of cereal and a glass of milk. He was careful not to choose Crummies. Scotty settled for three doughnuts and milk.

"Where are the girls?" Rick asked. "Still asleep?"

"They've gone swimming," Mrs. Morrison replied. "They should be back soon, though. They've been gone over an hour."

"I could use a swim myself," Rick admitted.

"Not me," Scotty said. "Wait until afternoon and I'll join you. That cold water would shock me into a state of galloping goose pimples the way I feel now."

Rick had forgotten how cold the water was. "Okay. We'll wait. Let's go over to the lab and take down the lights. I want to clean up the trash cans, too."

They walked leisurely over to the laboratory and stopped for a moment to chat with Joe Blake. Then, before starting on the lights, they walked around behind the lab building.

The laboratories were built on a promontory that sloped inland toward Pirate's Field, which was just above sea level. The raised area ran around the seaward side of the island, so that the Brant house was on high land, too. On the north side, the land sloped down toward the boat landing.

Rick stood on the edge of the low cliff and looked for Barby and Jan. They weren't in sight.

"They must be using lungs," Scotty said. "Watch for bubbles."

No bubbles were visible, either. Rick checked carefully and began to worry. It was a calm day with little wave action, and the bubbles from the lungs should have been clearly visible. Surely they wouldn't swim so far the bubbles couldn't be seen on a day like this.

"Let's check," Rick said.

The boys hurried to the room where the Scuba equipment was kept. Two lungs and the blue and white equipment were gone. So was the cart. A quick look at Pirate's Cove showed no cart in sight.

Where could they have gone? The boys hurried to the front of the lab building again and found Joe Blake still getting a bit of sunshine.

"Did you see the girls?" Rick asked hurriedly.

Joe nodded. He motioned across the island. "They came and got aqualungs and hauled the cart across to the north side. They're probably swimming over there."

Rick doubted it. He doubted it very much. The currents on the north side kept the bottom stirred up and visibility was too poor for diving.

Without the need of exchanging a word, Rick and Scotty were suddenly running. As they passed the house Rick had a sudden thought. He went in and ran up the stairs to his room, grabbed his radio unit and turned it on.

"Barby!" he called frantically. "Barby!"

There was no answer. Tucking the unit into his pocket, he ran out and joined Scotty again. If Barby had her set she wasn't using it.

"Come on." He led the way to the boat cove and stopped short. The speedboat was there, and so was the Scuba cart, but the rowboat wasn't. Anxiously he scanned the water. There was no sign of the girls.

Where were they? Where? The thought struck him. He remembered Barby's comment of the night before.

Had they gone to the houseboat?

CHAPTER XVII

Pointer to Disaster

Scotty ran to the speedboat and yelled, "Come on!"

"Wait!" Rick called. "Let's not go barging off without knowing what we're doing."

Scotty turned, puzzled. "What do you mean?"

"The girls have some kind of plan, and we don't know what it is. If we go barging around in the speedboat, we might throw a monkey wrench into the works."

"But we can't just stand here and do nothing," Scotty said desperately.

"We won't. Go get the plane warmed up and wait for me."

Rick hurried into the house and ran up the stairs to Barby's room. Working fast, he went through the dresser, then through the shelves in her closet. Not finding what he wanted, he paused to look around in case he might have overlooked a possibility.

He didn't know where girls kept things, and he

suspected that sometimes the places weren't the same as boys might pick. But he could see no possible place that he hadn't searched.

That meant Barby had her Megabuck unit with her, unless she had left it somewhere else in the house.

He plugged in his earphone and called. "Barby!"

There was no reply. His lips set grimly. No use wasting time here. He ran from the house, hearing the sound of the Sky Wagon as Scotty warmed it up. Joe Blake was not in sight. Rick hurried into the lab and found him watching Professor Morrison who was checking some calculations on the lab's small computing machine.

"Joe, step outside with me for a moment, please."

Outside, Rick explained that the girls were missing, then asked, "Can you get the plane frequency on your receiver?"

"Sure. It's an all-wave job. What's the frequency you use?"

Rick told him, then explained, "We don't know what's going on, so we want to be prepared. If some of your Scout leaders can move down the coast to North Cove and keep an eye on the houseboat, Scotty and I will search from the air. If we see anything, we'll let you know on the plane's radio. You won't be able to talk back, but at least you can hear us, and you can let the Scouts know."

He wished his mind had worked faster. Then he could have taken Scotty's Megabuck unit and given it to Joe. But there was no time now, and this other arrangement probably would do as well.

"I'll pass the word to the gang on the mainland right away," Joe agreed.

Joe went back into the lab while Rick ran to Pirate's Beach. Scotty was waiting, the plane's engine turning over. Together, they launched the Sky Wagon, then climbed in, Scotty in the pilot's seat.

As Scotty took off, Rick tried Barby again on the radio. "Barby, this is Rick. Can you read me?"

There was no reply.

"Better fly as though we were heading for Whiteside," Rick suggested. He rubbed his palms on his handkerchief. They were damp with nervous perspiration. He was not as calm as he looked.

Scotty swung around on course and Rick scanned the water as they passed over the north side of Spindrift. There was no sign of the rowboat yet.

The plane traveled in a straight line right across North Cove. The houseboat was at anchor a few hundred yards offshore, and the pram was tied up to the rear rail. There was no sign of life.

The boys reached the Whiteside pier without seeing the girls or the boat. Scotty put the plane into a tight circle and looked at Rick helplessly. "Now what?"

"They can't have gone far," Rick mused. "Not in the rowboat."

"They had the aqualungs," Scotty pointed out. "They must have expected to use them."

"Right. But how? If they planned to get aboard the houseboat, they wouldn't be using the aqualungs. Or would they?"

"Search me."

"Wouldn't they just row up to the houseboat on some excuse or other? I wish I'd looked. Barby might have taken those clothes Dad wore home last night."

"We can't just float around and talk," Scotty said urgently. "Let's do something."

Rick felt the same way. "Okay. Throttle down and go slow. We'll scan the whole coastline from here to Spindrift."

Scotty did so, holding the little plane barely above stalling speed. Rick leaned out and traced the shore with anxious eyes.

The plane turned and twisted as Scotty followed the coastline as accurately as he could. They reached the upper tip of North Cove and swung into the cove itself.

Scotty tapped Rick on the shoulder and pointed. A man and a woman had come out of the houseboat and were watching the plane.

"Wonder where the other pair is?" Rick asked. There was nothing they could do about the people on the houseboat now. Let them wonder what the plane was doing. Rick turned his attention back to the shore below.

The plane traveled the length of the cove's shoreline and rounded the southern tip. They passed over a section where the woods came right down to the water. Birches leaned far over. Rick caught a glimpse of what might have been the rowboat, then the plane swung and he lost it.

"Circle," he said quickly. "I think I saw something!"

Scotty gunned the Sky Wagon and threw it into a tight turn. Rick watched carefully as the clump of birches came into view. There was a boat under them, all right. He wished for the binoculars, but they were probably at the attic lookout where Barby and Jan had spied on the houseboat.

He had no real doubt. He was sure the boat was the Spindrift rowboat.

"Circle over the island," he called to Scotty, then reached over and took the hand microphone from the instrument panel rack. He turned on the radio and waited a moment while it warmed.

"Joe, this is Rick," he said. "Rowboat under a clump of birches just south of North Cove. Have the boys go there and look it over. See if the girls are in the woods. We'll watch for sign of the girls on the water."

To Scotty, he directed, "Over the cove. Circle the whole area. We'll watch for their bubbles. Joe's men will check the woods."

The plane turned obediently. Presently they were moving in a wide circle with the houseboat as a center. A slight surface wind had arisen and the water in the cove was a bit choppy, but not enough to obscure bubble tracks made by Scuba divers below.

"See anything?" Rick asked.

"Not a trace. Can you see the water around the houseboat well enough?"

"Yes. No bubbles in the vicinity." Rick dried his palms again, then mopped his forehead. He was becoming thoroughly frightened. Where were they?

He checked his Megabuck radio to be sure it was on and called, "Barby. Where are you?"

The air was silent, except for the slight background hiss that was always present.

"Look right under the houseboat's gunwales," Scotty urged. "If they're directly under it, the bubbles would rise along the sides."

"Why would they go under the houseboat?" Rick asked.

Scotty shook his head. "Why did they come over here in the first place?"

Rick had no answer. "Let's go over to the shore. Joe's men ought to be at the rowboat by now. Maybe they found the girls."

Scotty banked around and headed over the clump of birches. In a small clearing behind the clump they saw two men in Scout uniforms. The men looked up, and one spread his hands wide in a gesture that said nothing of importance had been turned up.

"There's only one thing to do," Rick said decisively. "We've got to check on the . . ."

He stopped as though a hand had clutched his throat. Barby's voice, in his earphones!

POINTER TO DISASTER 185

Rick pulled the unit from his pocket and turned up the volume. He couldn't hear her well.

"It's Barby," he said swiftly. "Circle!"

Rick strained to hear. She was talking to someone. ". . . It won't do the slightest bit of good to keep us here, because my brother will know where we are."

The signal faded as she talked. Rick turned the little radio unit, trying to keep the volume constant.

"You'd better let us go," Barby was saying. "You'll get into a lot of trouble if you don't."

Rick groaned. Her threats would do about as much good as a bunny threatening a wolf pack. Where was she? On the houseboat?

Suddenly he realized . . . he had the key in his hands!

Barby's voice was high-pitched and frightened now. "What are you doing? Why are you putting that plastic cap on Jan?"

Rick turned the radio unit as the plane circled. The sweat stood out on his face. Unerringly, the axis of the built-in antenna pointed to the houseboat.

There was no longer any doubt!

"Land!" he yelled. "Land next to the houseboat!"

Scotty slammed the throttle in instant response, and as the Sky Wagon dived toward the water he cast a quick look at Rick. "What did you hear?"

Rick was already slipping off his shoes, getting ready to jump. "On the houseboat!" he choked. "They're using the mind reader on the girls!"

CHAPTER XVIII

The One-Man Boarding Party

Scotty hit the water and bounced once, but he held the plane down and in a moment the water slowed it. He revved up again and taxied as rapidly as he dared to the houseboat, swung broadside to it, and throttled back.

Rick was waiting. He flung the door open and dove far enough to clear the pontoon. The cold water closed over him briefly, then with a powerful kick he flashed to the surface again. A few strokes brought him to the houseboat.

The two men were leaning on the rail. One, a hefty man of middle age with a striped shirt and glasses, said politely, "Do you want something?"

Rick stopped and tread water. "I want the two girls you have inside. Have them come out here, and we won't bother you any more."

The second man, the dark-haired one who had

come to Spindrift, smiled. "You mean our wives? They're having a nap. Sorry."

"I mean my sister and her friend. Stop stalling, Mister."

Striped shirt shook his head. "Sorry, boy. We haven't seen your sister. Now climb back on your little airplane and get out of here."

Rick's reply was a stroke that brought him to the houseboat. He reached up for a handhold, when a boat hook suddenly touched his forehead.

"Don't try it," striped shirt said. "Stay off this barge or I'll bend this pole over your head. Now get out of here."

Rick back-pedaled helplessly. Now what? He knew there was no possibility of his climbing aboard while the men were on deck.

And what was happening inside? He swam forward, to the front of the boat, and the men followed. They could move faster than he; there was no possibility of outdistancing them.

If only he had a weapon! But wishing was useless. He had to do something! He called, "Barby! Can you hear me?"

There was no answer from inside. His pulse speeded. Were Barby and Jan all right, perhaps gagged, or had the mind reader already worked?

Rick swam away from the houseboat a few feet and floated, his mind racing. There had to be a way of getting aboard. There had to!

Where was Scotty? He listened, and heard the

plane's engine on the other side of the houseboat. In a few seconds Scotty came into view. He was on the water close to shore, traveling at high speed. As Rick watched, Scotty swung the plane on a line with the houseboat and opened the throttle wide.

Rick stared. Was his pal out of his mind? If he crashed the houseboat, the girls would be hurt, too! Then he realized Scotty would never pull such a stunt, no matter how desperate he became.

The men on the houseboat were at the rail now, eyes on the racing plane. In that instant Rick divined Scotty's plan, he hoped, and turned to gauge his distance. The plane was on the upper step now, almost air-borne. Even as he watched, the pontoons pulled away. But Scotty held the plane on the water, roaring propeller pointed right at the men at the rail.

Rick put his head down and sprinted for the front of the houseboat. He had to time it perfectly!

To the horrified eyes of the men at the rail a collision was inevitable. They could only assume that the madman in the plane was going to smash right into them. And as Scotty had planned, they lost all interest in Rick, in the presence of immediate, personal danger.

The men threw themselves to the deck, clawing frantically for some kind of cover. At the last instant, Scotty pulled the plane up in a power climb. So near disaster had he come that the suction of the passing pontoons lifted a coiled rope into the air on

"Stay away or I'll bend this pole over your head!"

top of the cabin. Even as he mounted the rail and stood on deck, Rick gave a prayer of thanks for his pal's perfect judgment and lightning reflexes.

He ran along the deck, jumped over the two prostrate men, swung around and launched himself into the cabin. He stopped, eyes wide with fright.

Barby was lashed to a chair just inside the door, a gag in her mouth. Jan was on the other side of the cabin, also lashed. But Jan had a plastic cap on her head, and wires ran from it to a machine on a nearby table. Two women were standing over the girl, and one had a pistol in her hand.

Rick started forward, then stopped helplessly. The pistol wasn't pointed at him. It was pointed at Jan's head!

He looked into Jan's pleading eyes and shifted his weight uncertainly. He didn't know what to do now.

Jan did. Her arms were lashed tight, but her legs were free. She lifted one of them in a kick that caught the pistol-holding woman behind the knees. The pistol hand lifted as the woman flailed for balance, and Rick sprang like a charging fullback. His widespread arms embraced both women and slammed them back into the cabin wall. Then he scrambled to his feet in search of the gun. It was under Jan's chair. He bent to pick it up when Barby gave a muffled cry from behind the gag. Rick whirled.

The two men were rushing him from the cabin entrance.

THE ONE-MAN BOARDING PARTY 191

There wasn't much room in the cabin, but it gave Rick an advantage. He dove toward the men, who stopped their rush briefly. But Rick hadn't made the dive with the intention of meeting them head on. There was a table along the wall next to the corner where Barby was tied up. Rick went under it.

The men rushed for the table. Rick reached out and grabbed an ankle. Bracing his legs, he gave a mighty heave. Striped shirt went over backward in front of Barby, who stamped with both bare feet on his stomach. The breath went out of him with a whoosh.

Rick gathered his legs and shoved upward. The table heaved into the other man and threw him off balance long enough to give Rick a chance to get to his feet. Keeping the table between him and the dark man, Rick watched for an opening. Striped shirt was on his knees, shaking his head.

The dark man was tired of waiting. He launched himself across the table, arms outstretched. It was the best move he could have made, from Rick's point of view. The boy knew he could not compete with either man in strength. He had to depend on speed, and the infighting tricks he had learned from Scotty. He used one now. At the last moment he side-stepped and his hand flashed down. It was a judo chop, the hand held stiff, the blow delivered with the side opposite the thumb. It was effective. The man dropped to the floor, shaking his head. Rick used the *savate,* the blow delivered with the heel. It landed against the side of the man's neck. He went over sideways.

Striped shirt was on his feet now, but still starved for air. His mouth hung open as he gasped, but he was coming forward.

Rick met him. He dove into the man's stomach and felt his head smack into soft flesh. The breath went out of striped shirt again. Rick regained his feet and turned to Barby. She was making sounds through her gag, her eyes desperate.

The boy whirled. The women were back in the fight, one of them scrambling for the gun under Jan's chair. Jan kicked it far back, out of reach. Rick scooped up the table and slid it along the floor at them. The table caught them like a pair of tenpins and knocked them into the corner. He turned back to Barby and started to untie her, his fingers racing.

A blow landed on his shoulder. He turned in time to meet another one across the cheek that knocked him back against the wall. He rebounded, fighting. The dark man was crouched low, fists weaving. Rick danced lightly around him waiting. Let the man come to him.

The man led with a right. Rick rolled away from it, watching the left that was cocked for a Sunday punch. The man threw his punch. Rick caught it on the forearm and gasped with the pain of it. The guy had a wallop like a mule!

Rick feinted with the hurt arm, then drove a chop at the man's nose. It connected and brought a gasp of pain. Barby was screaming through the gag again, but he couldn't look now. He brought a roundhouse punch up under his opponent's guard and felt it smack solidly against ribs. Then an arm encircled his neck and a clenched fist crashed against the back of his head. He saw stars, and for a moment his guard dropped. Then both arms were pinioned.

Striped shirt had caught him from behind. Now the dark man stepped in, fist cocked for a knockout punch. Rick saw it coming and braced himself.

The punch never landed. A crisp voice said, "Don't do it!"

Encircling arms fell away. Rick turned, knees weak.

A man in Boy Scout uniform stood in the cabin door, and in his hand was a Police Positive.

"All right," the Scout said cheerfully. "Party's over."

CHAPTER XIX

Taped for Trouble

ANOTHER Scout leader moved into the cabin, followed by Scotty. Rick gave them a grin, then turned and picked up the gun behind Jan's chair. He stuck it in his pocket and untied the girl.

The plastic cap was still on her head. He lifted it off gently and put it on top of the machine.

"Are you all right?" he asked.

She nodded, hand at her throat. "Yes," she managed. "I can't talk. The gag . . ."

"Time for talk later," Rick said. He started for Barby, but Scotty was already untying her. The moment her hands were free, she pulled the gag from her mouth and announced, "Well! You took long enough getting here!"

Rick didn't know what to say to that. He didn't have a chance to say anything. His sister rushed over, put her arms around him, and squeezed.

"You were wonderful," she said. "Scotty, he held

four of them at bay. I never knew you could fight like that, Rick Brant!"

Rick grinned. "I didn't do so much. You took one of them out of play by stamping on him. And Jan gave me an opening with as fine a kick as I've seen off a football field."

The two JANIG agents had produced handcuffs, and the men and women were manacled together in a continuous chain.

"Outside," one agent commanded. "Get into the pram."

"You've got nothing on us," the man in the striped shirt protested. "We were only protecting ourselves against this wild man who barged in here."

"Were you protecting yourselves against the two girls?" Scotty asked.

"We were holding them for the police," striped shirt stated. "They sneaked aboard, probably intending to steal anything they could find. You're going to get yourselves into a peck of trouble, my friends. There's a law in the state against carrying firearms! A fine reputation this will give the Boy Scouts!"

The agent with the pistol said mildly, "You talk too much. Get in the pram." To Rick he said, "We're taking them to Spindrift. We'll send the speedboat back for you."

The four young people stood at the rail and watched as the crowded pram with its outboard motor chugged off to the island.

Barby pulled off her bathing cap, and Rick saw that she wore the Megabuck unit underneath. He pointed to it. "I tried to call you. Why didn't you answer?"

Barby replied with an embarrassed blush that started at the shoulders and swept up until her face was bright red. "I forgot to turn it on," she admitted. "Jan reminded me while they were tying her up. They hadn't got to me, yet. One of the women was holding the pistol and pointing it at me. Jan sort of looked up and said, 'We need an outside power to help us now. But we must be sure the power is turned on.' Then I remembered. I pretended my head hurt, and pushed the switch."

Rick looked at Jan. "That was clever. I'd been trying to reach Barby, with no success. Then, suddenly, I heard her talking."

"We knew you were close, because we could hear the plane." Jan shuddered. "The men heard it, too, because they ran out right after they tied us up and put that thing on my head. The women guarded us, and one of them had just started the machine running when the plane came right at us. We saw it, through the open door, and we thought you were going to crash!"

Rick grinned at Scotty. "That was our fast-acting pal. If he hadn't done that, I'd never have had a chance to get aboard."

"Good thing you figured out what I was doing," Scotty admitted. "When I saw you moving fast toward the boat, I knew it was okay, and that I didn't have to crash."

Rick stared. "Do you mean you'd have actually crashed?"

"Not head on, because that would have hurt the girls. I was planning to swing at the last minute and try to knock the men off with the wing."

Rick could only mutter, "My sainted aunt!"

Scotty turned on the girls. "And here's the pair that made it necessary. What in the name of a painted parsnip were you two trying to do?"

Barby lifted her chin defiantly. "We had a good plan. Can we help it if it didn't work?"

"Can't answer that until we know the plan," Scotty said reasonably. "Suppose you tell us."

"Well, we needed evidence that the houseboaters were in the plot against our fathers, didn't we? I knew we could get it, if we could plant a radio. So we made a plan."

"Lot of good a turned-off radio would have done," Rick muttered.

Barby glared. "We decided that we'd go swimming with the lungs. Then we'd come up right next to the houseboat, and we'd be so surprised! Of course the people would come out to see us, then we'd say I had a cramp, and could we please come up and rest."

Rick listened, and he had to admit it wasn't a bad plan at all—so far.

"Of course they would let us rest. Then I'd wait

for a chance to put the radio behind a cushion, or in the crack of an armchair, or somewhere like that. I didn't know exactly what I could do, but I knew if we could get aboard there would be some way of leaving the radio behind."

The pram had vanished around the turn of the cove. The speedboat would come into sight any moment now.

"All right," Rick admitted. "Let's say it was a good plan. What happened?"

Jan took up the tale. "We didn't want to try to swim all the way from Spindrift, so we took the rowboat and did exactly what Cap'n Mike did yesterday. We rowed along the shore with the aqualungs and got into the water right where we could see the houseboat. We had to. Otherwise, we would have gotten lost underwater."

"But you had the wrist compasses, didn't you?" Scotty asked. The boys had stressed that compasses were essential because low visibility in the waters off Spindrift made it very easy to lose one's sense of direction.

"We had the compasses," Barby said. "How do you think we swam right to the houseboat?"

"Then why didn't you get into the water out of sight of the houseboat?" Rick asked, and suddenly he knew. That would have meant plotting a compass course around a turn. So many feet in one direction, then change to another compass heading. He had explained it to them, but they just hadn't learned.

It was not easy, he had to admit, and it took practice even on land. "Never mind," he said. "I know the answer. Go ahead. Tell us the rest."

Barby studied his face. "I guess you do know," she assented. "Well, they told us later, on the houseboat. They saw us get into the water, then they watched our bubbles come right toward them. So when we got here, they weren't fooled."

"We went through with it, as we planned," Jan said, "and we thought we were getting away with it. They were very nice. Of course we could come up and rest. They were glad to have us stop by. But when we got aboard, one of the women had a gun, and she made us go into the cabin and sit down. Then they started asking us questions."

"What kind of questions?" Rick inquired.

"About why we had come. We stuck to the story, until they told us they'd seen us. Even then we didn't admit anything. Then Barby started to threaten them."

Scotty chuckled. "I'd like to have heard that."

Rick watched the tip of the cove. The speedboat from Spindrift should be coming shortly. "How about the plane?" he asked suddenly. "What did you do with it?"

Scotty motioned to the other side of the houseboat. "It's anchored. I landed next to the JANIG team and got into the rowboat with them." The Sky Wagon carried a small anchor and a few yards of anchor line in one of the pontoons.

"Okay. Carry on, Barby. How did you threaten them?"

"I was very logical," Barby stated. "Wasn't I, Jan?"

Jan nodded agreement. "You definitely were."

"I started by telling them that they couldn't possibly do a thing to us, and they might as well let us go right away."

"Bet that impressed them," Rick murmured.

"Are you telling this, or am I?"

"You are," Rick said contritely. "Go ahead."

"Well, I said my brother knew where we were, and they'd better be careful. It didn't work. Then I pointed out that they didn't even dare to kill us, because our bodies could be traced back to the houseboat. Everyone knew we'd just gone for a swim, and everyone knew we could take care of ourselves."

Rick thought privately that any time Spindrift was in danger from then on, he'd make sure his self-reliant sister had a bodyguard at all times.

"I said other things, too, but finally they slapped me and told me to shut up."

"Who did?" Scotty demanded.

"One of the women. It doesn't matter, Scotty. It didn't hurt. Anyway, they said we could stop worrying about what was going to happen to them. Then one of the men asked if we knew what had happened to the three scientists. We said yes. And he said . . . he said . . ." Barby suddenly turned white.

Jan finished for her. "He said they were going to erase our minds, too. Then they were going to put us back in the water." The words were no sooner out than Jan had a delayed reaction, too.

Rick rushed the two of them into the cabin and made them sit down with heads bent low. Scotty found water and gave them each a drink.

"You've acted like a couple of champs," Rick told them. "But for the love of mike, don't faint now!"

Barby lifted her chin. "I have no intention of fainting," she said defiantly. "It's just . . . well, it's . . ."

"I know," Rick assured her. "Take it easy, Sis."

He looked up. The sound of a racing speedboat was echoing inside the cabin. Good. They'd be home in a few minutes and his mother could take over. He gave the girls a comradely grin. What a pair!

The machine on the table attracted his eye. He walked over and studied it. The recording drum had wavy lines on it, probably the beginning of Jan's brain pattern. It made no sense to him, but it would to Parnell Winston.

"They had you taped," he told the girl gently. "But you saved your own bacon by telling Barby to turn on the radio. If you hadn't . . ."

A shudder ran through Jan's slim body. "I was taped for trouble. I'm glad you came through the door when you did!"

Rick's finger traced a line on the recording drum. "I'm kind of glad myself," he admitted.

CHAPTER XX

JANIG Closes In

STEVE AMES walked around the objects on the laboratory table. "Nothing deadly looking about these gadgets," he said. "Which goes to show how misleading appearances can be."

The objects included the barber's massage machine, an ancient composition-board suitcase, the gadget from the houseboat, and a TV set with an indoor antenna of the kind known as "rabbit ears."

Parnell Winston admitted, "There is plenty we don't know about them, especially the inside of that TV set. But we'll learn."

Steve smiled at the assembly of faces. In addition to the project team and the boys, Mrs. Brant, Mrs. Morrison, and the two girls were in the group. So was Joe Blake.

Rick regretted that Jerry, Duke, and Cap'n Mike could not be invited. But the matter was still not for discussion with people on the outside. If a story ever could be made public, the *Morning Record* would be the first to have it, but in all probability the facts would remain buried for some time.

In a large room in the lab basement the four houseboaters and the barber waited under heavy guard for the arrival of a Coast Guard cutter. The barber was there courtesy of Captain Douglas, who had picked him up and delivered him to Spindrift after a call from Joe Blake.

Steve rapped for attention. "We're about to tie up some loose ends, everyone. Let's get seated, because the cutter will be here any moment."

The room was sometimes used for lectures when Hartson Brant got his entire staff together, and there were plenty of chairs. In a moment the audience was seated comfortably and listening to Steve.

"You were all involved," the agent began, "so I want you all to know what has been going on. Some details are not known to us, yet. But we're continuing the investigation. However, the part that involves you is finished, and you'll probably never hear about the rest of it."

Rick knew that was true. Who the houseboaters and the barber really were, who paid them, how they had been tipped off to the project in the first place, and similar details would remain locked in top-secret files somewhere in Washington.

"The key to the whole affair was uncovered in Washington yesterday. Most of you know about the physical arrangements on the fourth floor. In setting up the security system we checked all wiring, traced all phone lines, and in general made sure the place was not 'bugged,' which is the term we use for wire taps, hidden microphones, and so on."

Steve paused, and Rick thought his friend looked a little embarrassed. "In spite of our care, it developed that we did have a hidden microphone picking up all conversation and relaying it to the enemy group. I can only say in our own defense that it was the kind of 'bug' we couldn't have found without tearing the building apart."

"It's nearly impossible to take all modern electronic developments into account," Julius Weiss said. "We all know how thorough you are, Steve. Go on."

"Thank you, Julius. Directly above us, on the fifth floor, was the Peerless Brokerage Company. It was a legitimate firm, doing a good business. We had no reason to suspect it, even though we checked out all firms both above and below us. Well, in checking on the houseboaters, we discovered that the firm had recently been taken over by a dummy corporation, and most of it was actually owned by the man Rick called 'striped shirt.' He bought the stock right after the project moved in on the fourth floor."

"There was no change in the firm?" Dr. Morrison asked. "Nothing suspicious?"

"Nothing. The firm continued to operate as always. There was one personnel change. A lawyer, representing the new principal stockholder, took over one of the offices."

Rick suspected that said lawyer was now in custody.

"As soon as we discovered the connection, we made a check. Under the floor in the lawyer's office we found a 'bug.' A hole had been drilled into the floor structure until only a thin shell of plaster remained. The plaster was, of course, our ceiling. So actually the microphone was within a fraction of an inch of our room, but there was no way we could detect it. That's how every move we made was anticipated, and why the enemy moved to Whiteside on the same day that the project moved to Spindrift."

That explained a lot, Rick thought. "Did the barber tape the two scientists?" he asked.

"We think so. He's the boss of the enemy team, Rick. We've found that during the period when he was in Washington, his massage machine was wired through to a room in the basement. The wiring went through the power cord into the electric outlet, and the impulses were actually transmitted over the power system and taken out of a plug in the basement. We found the machine where he had stored it."

Rick knew that could be done quite simply. The frequencies of the electric current and the brain patterns were so different that they would not interfere with each other.

"He didn't plan to use his machine in Whiteside," Steve went on, "because he left the mind-reading part of the machine in Washington."

"Then why did he bring it?" Barby asked.

"We're not sure. The likeliest possibility is that he wanted to continue using it as a massage machine, because he made a little money with it. I never knew an espionage agent who didn't need money."

Steve looked at Rick. "I'm a little surprised at one thing. Why didn't the Spindrift twins suspect foul play when Hartson Brant ran over something in the speedboat?"

It was Rick's turn to be embarrassed. "I guess we were so upset we didn't think straight. Why?"

"The mainland team found a log. It had a yoke on it. Apparently the houseboaters had taken a lesson from the incident on the pier and were waiting for Spindrift traffic on the water. We think they waited until they heard the sound of the Spindrift speedboat, then took the pram and cut across the course hauling a log on a long rope."

Scotty spoke up. "That's what puzzles me, Steve. Why the switch from long-distance electronics to violence?"

"When we moved the project to Spindrift, we also removed the chance of taping project members in some natural setting like the barbershop. They had hoped to knock out the team without anyone suspecting it was enemy interference. That worked, at first. But moving the project upset their plans. They rigged the train deal that caught Marks. But even though it worked, it showed we were dealing with an enemy."

"So they had to catch the scientists in order to tape them," Scotty commented.

"Right. Of course they tried to do it in a way that looked natural in the case of Marks and Dr. Brant. Probably they hoped the attack on Duke, whom they mistook for Morrison, would be taken as a holdup. They undoubtedly planned to allow time between the accident, or attack, and following through with the mind-reading machine, hoping that the two wouldn't be connected."

The pattern was clear, Rick thought. Like many such schemes, the moment a suspicion of foul play developed, the plan began to boomerang.

"I think the order of events is clear enough," Steve concluded. "Any questions?"

Barby had one. "I don't understand about Dr. Marks. Did they turn on the mind reader from the train?"

"Probably. The man on the train apparently had a two-section gadget in a suitcase. One part took the EEG and the other sent out the signal that did the damage. He waited until the train was pulling out of the station before turning on the record section. Then all he had to do was get off at New York. We haven't found him, or his machine. But we will. Any other questions?"

"Why did the barber move to Whiteside, if he didn't intend to tape anyone?" Weiss asked.

"The barbershop in any small town is a good central location for keeping track of goings-on in town.

I think that's all he had in mind—besides the fact that barbering was his trade. If Vince Lardner hadn't needed an assistant, he probably would have moved into one of the summer colonies, or gotten some other kind of job. We can't be sure."

Rick asked, "Are there any machines in existence besides these two and the missing one from the train?"

"We don't know. But it doesn't matter. The enemy now knows we're onto the system and can't expect to get away with it again. Besides, Dr. Winston says a countermeasure is easily arranged, to be used when we suspect the mind readers might make another try."

"Who are these people?" Jan demanded.

Steve grinned. "Unfriendly agents. Seriously, Jan, we aren't sure about their employers. It will take some backbreaking investigation to get the whole story, because the files show nothing on any of them. That means they were deep-cover agents, kept hidden until there was something important enough to bring them out. We may never get the whole story."

"Won't they talk?" Scotty asked.

"They haven't yet. They may. But, anyway, we'd have to check on their stories. Any other questions? Okay, I'm finished. Dr. Winston will take over at this point."

The cyberneticist came to the front of the room. "We have something here," he stated, "but we don't yet know what it is. And, curiously enough, from the crude nature of the machines, I doubt that the enemy knows, either. If we have to speculate—and I guess we do—we might guess that sometime, in an enemy EEG laboratory, some experiment resulted in a subject having his mind erased. It was probably an accident that the enemy exploited without knowing how it worked."

"Can't we even guess how it works?" Weiss asked.

"Approximately, without knowing the physiology of it. The EEG recording is simply fed into a gadget that modulates a carrier wave. The carrier is an average frequency for brain patterns. In effect, the thing simply transmits the man's own pattern back to him. Why that should produce trauma of the kind we have seen is a mystery." The scientist gestured to the TV receiver. "The transmitter is incorporated into the TV chassis, and the 'rabbit ears' act as an antenna when adjusted properly. The recorder is a simple EEG mechanism."

Winston smiled. "You may be sure we're not through with this apparatus. I'm leaving the project immediately to set up a new team with Chavez, for the investigation of this phenomena. It may be another major key to the physiology of the brain."

"Do you mean we know nothing more than you've told us?" Rick asked.

"Nothing more, Rick. Oh, are you wondering about the barber's machine? Actually, the massage gadgets acted as electrodes, and the massage oil did very well in making good contact. It was a simple setup."

There were no questions for Parnell Winston. Steve took over. "In a short time we'll take the prisoners off your hands. Joe Blake and two men will remain as guards, but I think we have nothing more to worry about beyond routine security."

"I just remembered," Rick interrupted. "How about the elevator operator?"

"We picked him up, but he didn't know a thing. The barber paid him in free haircuts to keep track of people coming and going from the fourth floor. That's all. He didn't know why."

Joe Blake came in the door. "Motor whaleboat coming, Steve. Shall we take the prisoners to the landing?"

"Yes, Joe. Please."

Barby looked at Steve speculatively. "How about the houseboat?"

"Well, how about it? Haven't you seen enough of it?"

Barby smiled. "It would be very nice, if it were only another color. What will happen to it?"

"A coast guardman will be after it tomorrow. It will be impounded for a while. After that it may be sold for public auction, or it may revert to the owner's estate. It depends on the court."

Barby looked a little disappointed. "Oh, well, we don't really need a houseboat, anyway."

The group broke up as Joe and his partner walked the prisoners across the island to the landing. In a short time the motor whaleboat was speeding to the horizon where a cutter waited.

Rick took a last look. That just about closed the case. The remaining details probably would never be known to the Spindrift group.

"Can't anything be done for Dr. Marks and the other scientists?" he asked Parnell Winston.

Winston shook his head. "No, Rick. We're afraid to tamper, for fear of making things worse. But I neglected to tell you one very important item. The first scientist stricken is becoming rational again, or at least we hope so. Yesterday he asked for food. A short time later he picked up a pencil and paper and began to work out an equation, one connected with the project. Apparently the equation was the last thing he had been working on when the mind reader struck. So we hope and believe that nature is healing the damage. There is no evidence of tissue destruction, so perhaps complete recovery is possible. It's a question of waiting and watching."

Within two weeks Rick had an opportunity to see for himself, because the two scientists from Washington joined the Spindrift group. They were fully recovered, with only vague memories of the period when their minds were not functioning. And Dr. Marks was reported well on the way to normalcy.

The project was almost at an end, with only a few final checks needed on the critical equations. The Morrisons had already set a day for their departure— to Barby's great unhappiness.

As Barby said at dinner one night, "I didn't realize how lonely it gets sometimes without another girl on the island. Until Jan came, that is. Now she's going, and I wish she weren't."

"I'd love to stay," Jan said. "Really I would."

Hartson Brant arrived in time to hear the last exchange. He had left the table briefly to take a phone call. "I'm afraid it's going to be pretty quiet on Spindrift," he agreed. "It looks as though we'll be losing Rick and Scotty for a while!"

Barby wailed, "Not again! Why can't they stay home for a while?"

Rick and Scotty had looked up with quick interest at the scientist's words.

"We've been home for weeks," Rick replied. His eyes were on the slip of paper in his father's hand. "Dad, what is it? Where are we going?"

"Read it aloud," Hartson Brant suggested. He handed Rick the slip.

Rick scanned it quickly. It was a telegram that his father had taken over the phone. Rick's pulse quickened. Dr. Gordon, who had been at work on a secret rocket project in the far west, had wired:

> ARRIVING TOMORROW. NEED RICK AND SCOTTY FOR SPECIAL WORK. URGE THEY BE READY TO DEPART IN THREE DAYS EQUIPPED FOR EXTENDED STAY AT DESERT BASE.

Rick's eyes met Scotty's as he finished reading. "Desert base," he repeated.

Scotty grinned his delight. "John Gordon's rocket base is in the desert. He must want us there."

"But why?" Barby demanded. "You're not rocket experts. Why, even when we had the moon rocket here, you didn't work on the rocket itself."

That was perfectly true. Rick shrugged. "You know as much as we do, Sis."

Hartson Brant stirred his coffee thoughtfully. "I have a hunch," he said. "From the tone of the wire, I suspect John is in some kind of difficulty. Surely he doesn't want you as technicians, but it's not beyond the bounds of possibility that he needs a little detective work done."

It made sense to Rick. But what kind of detective work could he and Scotty do at a highly guarded and secret government base? He fought down the impulse to run up to his room and start packing. Gordon had said in three days. There was plenty of time. Except that Rick knew he'd be dizzy with wondering until John Gordon gave them more information.

The Morrisons rose to the occasion beautifully. "We wouldn't want Barby to be without any companions of her own age here," Mrs. Morrison said quickly. "If it's all right, I'm sure we can let Jan remain until the boys return."

The girls beamed without saying a word, then they broke into excited chatter. Rick and Scotty retired to the front porch and grinned at each other.

"If Dad is right, this is going to be plenty of fun," Scotty said happily. "I've always wanted to get close to the big rockets."

"We'll find out," Rick said. "And if John Gordon has a mystery, we're the pair who can solve it for him."

Later, Rick's words returned to him under the most unusual and terrifying circumstances of his entire life. The story of the project that led to Rick's greatest adventure will be told in the next Rick Brant Science-Adventure mystery.